touch

by Charlotte Watson Sherman

Fiction
One Dark Body
Killing Color

Anthology
Sisterfire: Black Womanist Fiction and Poetry

touch

a novel

CHARLOTTE WATSON SHERMAN

HarperCollins*Publishers*

HarperCollins books may be purchased for educational, business, or sales promotional use. For information please write: Special Markets Department, HarperCollins Publishers, Inc., 10 East 53rd Street, New York, NY 10022.

FIRST EDITION

Designed by Caitlin Daniels

Library of Congress Cataloging-in-Publication Data
Sherman, Charlotte Watson, 1958–
   Touch : a novel / by Charlotte Watson Sherman. —1st ed.
      p.   cm.
   ISBN 0-06-016925-7
   I. Title.
PS3569.H415T68   1995
813' .54—dc20   95-21749

95 96 97 98 99 ❖/HC 10 9 8 7 6 5 4 3 2 1

We live in the age of fear—fear of difference, fear of violence, fear of darkness which we always ascribe to the other and never to ourselves. AIDS is our fear made visible. Pushing us ever into denial, it both taunts and challenges our humanity. For me it's not a fight against AIDS. It's a struggle against human weakness, that humanity might win out over fear.

—Barbara Earl Thomas,
N. W. AIDS Foundation,
Art Works for AIDS '95

part one

one

"*¿Qué pasa?*" Rayna turned toward the voice behind her.

"Don't look so surprised. I told you I was coming. Seen anyone exciting?"

Rayna shook her head as she watched her dear friend and collaborator, Novel Lewis, ignore the roomful of carefully constructed art pieces to seek out a potential lover.

"Our piece is on the third floor, in case you're interested."

"Yeah. Yeah. Yeah. I can't wait to see all that stainless steel and existential angst."

Rayna sighed and shook her head. Novel would never change.

"It's not like that, Novel. Just because we're in a health care facility, doesn't mean the art is going to be sterile."

"I hope the same holds true for some of these gorgeous men I've got my eyes on. They can't all be gay."

Rayna turned from Novel and walked over to the red-clothed table holding platters of frosted purple grapes, gleaming trays of Brie, Gouda, and goat cheese, plus dozens of cups of white wine.

After sliding a grape between her lips, Rayna decided to forgo her usual abstinence from alcohol. The cup of sparkling amber trembled slightly in her hands. She put it to her lips and took a long sip.

A man barked, then laughed a deep belly laugh. Rayna stared at him. He wore a blue plaid shirt beneath a brown leather bomber jacket. Once, the blue jeans he wore must've been tight. Now, they sagged at the hips and seat of his pants. The legs fit neatly over a pair of royal blue cowboy boots.

As Rayna watched, the man continued to laugh and gesture with fingers whose skin appeared pale and thin as translucent membranes.

A Timberline dancer, Rayna thought. Her best friend, C'Anne, had pointed out the group of square-dancing gay men who added a bit of gaiety to an otherwise somber occasion, as a chanting mass of people circled Myrtle Edwards Park during a walk to raise money for AIDS research. It had been Rayna's first year participating in the annual AIDS walk.

Those boots are a dead giveaway, Rayna thought. When she looked at the man's wasting face, she knew he was not at the reception as an artist.

Not far from Rayna, Sarita, a multimedia performance artist, stood with hands on hips in a heated discussion with a ceramics artist, Jesus Salazar.

Sarita looked like an eruption of white. An avalanche of gold-embroidered white cotton flowed from her tiny neck and swirled at her bronze slipper-clad feet. Silver dreadlocks coiled at the crown of her head. Her bone, shell, and bead earrings always made their own kind of music when Sarita walked. The two women nodded at each other.

Directly across from Rayna, an elderly couple stood clutching each other's arms. Their eyes were large and dark in their weathered faces. They stayed near the wall as if it could somehow protect them in the midst of all this. . . .

They must have a son here, Rayna thought. Rayna began to appreciate the reality of the chilly specter of AIDS circling the room, reaching into each corner, its evil dust swirling in every nook and crevice, brushing its icy fingertips across the heated temples of too many, searching for more, too many more to clutch to its empty bosom.

The Art from the Heart reception was the gala opening ceremony for Bailey-Boushay House, a state-of-the-art residential care facility for people disabled with AIDS. Artists had been invited to submit slides of their work for possible inclusion as installations in each of the patients' rooms. Rayna had been pleased, but surprised, that the ceramic tile collage she and Novel had created was selected to become a permanent part of the building.

"You'd never think this was a place where people are going to come to die," Novel whispered.

Novel was right. As Rayna looked at the circular column in the middle of the entrance lobby covered with bits of glass, stone, tile, marbles, playing cards, shells, beads, names, words, she couldn't help but marvel at the beauty of the creation.

"But what a place to die," Rayna whispered back.

The multitude of variations, the symmetry and colors and textures found inside Bailey-Boushay's walls were all the heaven Rayna could ever hope for if she ever needed to come to a place like this.

As a child from a working-class background, Rayna had not been exposed to art. But she had been an artist inside her heart from the day she could hold a stick and draw in the dirt. Rayna had lived her adult life as if there was nothing more important.

They had almost missed the opportunity to be a part of this art project. Novel had declined Rayna's first invitation to collaborate on a piece for Bailey-Boushay.

"An AIDS hospital? That is entirely too depressing for me!" Novel had declared.

"You're the one who's always asking about us collaborating on something. Plus, the piece needs to be in more than one medium and you know how good you are with tile. Come on. Here's our chance," Rayna had pleaded.

"But AIDS? Who's going to see our work? I need to get my name out there. What if people think I've got AIDS? The only people going inside that place won't have art on their minds."

"Who cares what people think, we're artists, right? We're not supposed to want to be safe. We're supposed to take risks and have courage. There's going to be a lot of publicity around this project, Novel. A lot of publicity and great exposure for our work. You're the one who's always talking about finding a way to get out of being a therapist."

"But is this the only way out? I don't have that kind of courage and I don't know if I want that kind of publicity. I don't even want to think about AIDS. One time I sat down and tried to list all the people I'd been to bed with and I got depressed."

"Was it a long list?"

"It depends on what you mean by long. I had to go back to high school and college and the disco days and getting married and divorced and since then . . . actually, the list was shorter than I thought. But that's no comfort when I start multiplying by ten years and probably the same amount of people on their lists and on and on and you can see why I don't want to create anything for an AIDS hospital. It could bring me bad luck."

"But think about how it would look inside your portfolio."

"Folio, polio," Novel had retorted. But in the end, she had also given in.

"Look at those NYC chicks. Don't they ever get tired of wearing all that black?" Novel said as she peered at a small knot of women dressed in black tights, black thick-soled shoes, and short, tight black dresses.

"Is that black lipstick? They look like they're from Paris or somewhere."

Novel snorted.

"That's what they want you Seattle hicks to think. I'm so glad I'm from L.A."

"They do add something to the mix besides all of this grunge."

"But don't you think it's excessive?"

"No, I think they look sophisticated."

"Bull. That's just strain from all the intellectualizing they think they have to do."

"It's called exercising the mind, Novel. Exercising the mind."

"They give me a headache. Anyway, there's another part of my anatomy that needs exercising."

"Leave it to you to be looking for love inside an AIDS hospital. You are one *psycho* therapist."

"Just 'cause these people are here doesn't mean they have AIDS. We're here and we don't have it."

Rayna quickly ducked behind Novel.

"Don't say anything. Don't look."

"What?"

"Here come Circe and Car."

"Why are you hiding from your parents?"

For a moment Rayna didn't respond. She looked at a jagged stone protruding from a nearby wall. The three white striated lines circling that rock reminded her of Car, Circe, and herself. It was an odd-shaped rock and comforted Rayna because the story of her family was not a particularly circular one.

The state had taken Rayna from her real mother when she was three years old. Took her and put her with a skinny woman who lived in a house out in the woods.

Whenever Rayna went to church with this skinny woman, who she discovered was to be her foster mother, the joyous but sad pictures of fat-cheeked angels smiling in her Sunday school books made Rayna cry.

Circe and Amilcar adopted Rayna a year later. They moved Rayna away from the woods and the skinny woman, away from the "City of Destiny," Tacoma, Washington, and implanted her square in the middle of their lives in Seattle.

Nobody called Amilcar by his proper name but Circe. Everybody else called him Car. So did Rayna.

"Car," she had cried when afraid of the shadows that inched across her walls at night or the white-lipped moon that peeked through the crack in the middle of her curtains.

"Car," she had screamed with delight when she painted ice cream mustaches on his face from her double-dipped vanilla ice cream.

Circe was a woman who rarely smiled. Her ginger-colored face often looked like the life had been sucked from it. Unlike Car, she did not play Go Fish, Speed, or later, Bid Whist with Rayna.

They had never told Rayna why Circe had not had children. They waited until she was seven to tell her that she was adopted. And only then because Randy Crawford, who the kids all called Crayfish due to his skinny hooked fingers, had yelled at her on the playground after she had beaten him at a good game of tetherball that Circe wasn't her mama and Car wasn't her daddy like she thought.

"Why did my mama leave me?" she would often ask.

"We don't know why, honey," Car had always told her. "We're just glad you're here."

Circe, though, had had more information.

"Your mother wasn't like most people, that's all. She got stuck somewhere with one foot in heaven and the other in hell. Your mama had her own way of looking at things. Her own way of being in this world. Her ways just didn't fit *the* way, that's all. It ain't nothing for you to worry about."

"But did she love me?" Rayna would ask.

"A woman like her didn't have no way of knowing how to love, baby."

"Circe, why you wanna tell the child something like that?" Car had asked.

"'Cause you see she's wondering about things, don't you? I don't want her to come up like I did always worrying on something and never getting no answers, except talk out of the Bible."

"Well, everybody know how to love and your mother just had her own funny kind of way, that's all."

Car's words had not been a comfort to Rayna.

She was twelve years old when she found out her mother had been mentally ill. And her own fear of the illness began to blossom inside her like a wildflower in Circe's garden.

For too long in her life, Rayna had hidden the pictures she drew from the eyes of those she felt would not understand. How many times had she heard Circe and her long-necked friends talking about some person who was different from them, like Cheese, a man who did not act in what they felt to be a mannish manner. He sewed his own neon-colored pencil-leg suits and stiff bow ties. He sat with the women during Labor Day picnics instead of slapping ivory dominoes on the card tables with the men. "How can you talk against a man with so much life inside him?" Car would ask Circe later, after her women friends had gone, their laughter trailing behind them like a foul-smelling cape.

No one they had ever known had been an artist. Ironers of clothes, scrubbers of floors, tenders of babies, yes. That type of work with their hands was known to them, not suspect.

And though they might be able to starch a pant crease within an inch of its life, or polish a floor on their knees with hands molding their family histories into the grain of gleaming wood floors that would never belong to them, or tenderly clean a naked baby's body with a reverence and perfection identical to a sculptor shaping the finest stone, they never would have the audacity to name their life's work art.

No one they had ever known to be different was sane as far as they were concerned.

"They say your mama liked to draw on things," Circe had once told Rayna.

Rayna had stopped drawing for a long time then. She did not want them to see her painting or drawing things like the crazy woman who was her mama.

By the time she was twenty-five, Rayna knew there would be no hiding from the reality that she wanted to be an artist no matter what anyone else thought. She didn't even care what her husband, Carl, thought. Carl, who definitely didn't understand why she refused to commit to a thirty-year stint at the post office or wherever else she could find steady employment, instead of the serial employment that was the reality of her life by then.

"What about a retirement plan? How are we ever going to be able to afford to have kids if you don't stay on a job for longer than a year at a time? What about vacations?" He would yell at her during their increasingly frequent arguments.

They had only been married five years. Rayna had had that many jobs in the same amount of time. Though at first she had been drawn to the stable aura Carl exuded, by the time they divorced, she was repulsed by him and any talk about investments, retirement, savings, children, or the future. By the time they had signed the divorce decree, Rayna felt as if she were being released from an early grave she had been forced into by the sheer weight of Carl's financial planning.

No one understood why she had divorced Carl.

"I don't know, girlfriend. He's a Black-Man-Working and can hold a decent conversation. All that talk about money isn't to try to hold you back, it's to help you get ahead. I know, 'cause I tell that husband of mine the same kinds of things. And he doesn't listen to me any more than you listen to Carl," C'Anne had told her after Rayna had announced she was going to divorce Carl.

"He's killing my spirit with all of that talk and he doesn't understand anything about my life. I don't care if he's a Black-Man-Working, I want a partner in life who respects me and what I do. Carl makes jokes all the time about artists. I'm tired of defending myself to my own husband."

"Just think about it, girl. Long and strong. This is a big step you're about to take. I don't want you to step off a cliff."

"I appreciate what you're saying, but I know in my heart what I've got to do. I just need somebody in my corner who will help see me through this."

"You know I'm going to be here for you, Rayna. No matter what happens. I like Carl and all, but if you say he's got to go, then he's got to go."

Circe had not been as compliant as C'Anne.

"What do you mean, divorce? You think being married is supposed to be easy? You're supposed to just waltz on up to the altar and say the words and then when you get tired or he starts to get on your nerves you just waltz on out? You think I didn't never wanna leave Amilcar? You think I didn't never have no fancies about some other kind of man, some other kind of life, where I can lay up on my behind and ain't nobody gonna say nothing to me one way or the other 'cause it's all gonna go my way? I know we taught you better than that. And for what? Scratching on a piece of paper? If you want to scratch, girl, scratch. You don't need to pay no man or nobody else no mind if that's what you want to do and you ain't hurting nobody. But you can't act like them words don't mean nothing, like they something you say and then turn around three times and the words'll disappear. I know I didn't teach you to be waiting on no man to come riding in on a big white horse to save you. You got to save yourself, but you don't do it by hurting nobody else. I don't care what you say. If you didn't wanna live by the words, you never shoulda stood up and said 'em. You lied. And can't nothing ever put that lie back in your mouth."

Circe had vowed never to attend another art show.

"You told me you was trying to find the truth in what you're doing with them pictures. How you gonna try to find truth on that paper and you can't even find it in your real life?"

Circe, always the practical, no-nonsense queen bee.

Once, when Rayna was fifteen and smelling herself, the whiff of the womanhood coming her way gave her the courage, and the nerve, to question Circe's authority.

"Well, I don't think I need to do all of the laundry, plus wash dishes and do homework when all of us are grown in this house and should be cleaning up after ourselves," Rayna had begun, hands on hips. "Plus, I have to go to my own job. I don't think it's fair."

Circe had given Rayna one of those Circe-looks and calmly told her, "There's all kinds of things ain't fair in this life, girl. But I'll tell you this, when I say you do something in my house, where I pay the bills and pay for your raggedy behind to go to that school you go to, then you do what I say no matter what you think. There's only one woman ruling this house, and that's this one. Can't two grown women live in the same house. Now when you get so grown that you can take care of yourself and your own bills, then that'll be the day you become the ruler of your own place. But there ain't never gonna be two queens in this hive."

Car would probably never understand Rayna's desire to become an artist, either. But if the truth be known, Rayna could be a ditch digger and it would be all right with Car, as long as she was happy.

This would be the first time in ten years that Rayna allowed Circe and Car to come to one of her art shows. The last one they had come to was shortly before Rayna had decided to divorce Carl Broussard. She closed her eyes to hold back the painful memories threatening to surface inside her mind.

Car and Circe had spotted Rayna and Novel and were now heading tentatively in their direction. Rayna stepped from behind Novel and waited patiently for her parents to reach them.

"Hey now. There's my big-time artist girl," Car boomed in his satiny baritone. He reached for Rayna and pulled her inside his arms. He smelled like Old Spice and his chin tickled Rayna's cheek where bits of stubble brushed her skin. She had forgotten how good it felt to be hugged by Car. She felt his strength blend with her strength as she stood inside the embrace of his large body's heat.

"Look who I brought with me, the old she-devil herself," Car said, laughing. "Made her eat all of them big old righteous mean words."

Though the relationship between the two women had been strained for years, Rayna still felt glad that Circe had come. She pulled Circe inside the protective arc of their encircled arms.

"Hey, what about me?" Novel asked petulantly.

The three stopped hugging and turned toward Novel.

"You better get yourself on in here, girl. We ain't got all day," Car said.

Novel inserted herself in the center of the threesome and threw up her arms.

"I feel like we're making a commercial about family values or something, like those Mormon commercials," she said, laughing. Rayna escaped the embrace and threw a grape at Novel's head. They all laughed.

"It looks like they're getting ready to start the officiating," Car said, nodding toward the center of the room.

"That's Ricky Adonio. He makes altars. I bought one of his pieces last year," Rayna said. "He's the one who called and told me about this art project."

"He looks like he's getting ready to say something."

Rayna peered anxiously in Ricky's direction. He had moved to the center of the meeting room. The shushing voices quieted as everyone focused their attention on Ricky.

Two hundred pairs of eyes were upon him as if they all had known this moment was coming but had been willing to hold it at bay with their dying breaths if necessary.

Ricky stood as slender as a prepubescent girl in his well-

worn black Levis and black T-shirt. His large dark eyes were
two drops of chocolate inside a luminescent milk. His rich
brown skin stretched over his high, sharp cheekbones
reminded Rayna of the Cherokee on her mother's side.
Except for those shadows inside the hollows of his cheeks.
Her family didn't have those.

Rayna was surprised at the gauntness of Ricky's face, the
thinness of his body. He had not been that thin the last
time she saw him a little over one year ago.

This was a man who once bragged about his ability to
bench-press two hundred pounds. Now he didn't look as if
he could lift his arm to wave good-bye.

Rayna felt an urgent need to leave. She turned to whisper to Novel, but Ricky's ratchety whisper stilled her lips.
She turned toward the sound of that awful scratching as it
poured from Ricky in waves of rage. He stood with his feet
planted wide and his tight brown fists raised in the air as if
he would find God there and strike that timeless, sacred
face with the points of his bony knuckles until they were
covered with blood.

No one said a word.

The hair at the back of Rayna's neck stood on end. She
felt an overwhelming desire to escape the room but she
couldn't move. She was trapped inside Ricky's net of anger.

"I've got to get out of here. I can't breathe," Novel said.

Still no one moved.

Suddenly, Ricky's voice clearly filled the room, shocking
Rayna with its intensity.

"You can't come in here and leave as if nothing has happened. As if nothing is happening. As if everything hasn't
changed. Real people are coming here to die. Their deaths

will be real. This is not a car crash where you can stop your car for a moment and see if blood really flows from a wound. People with lives and hopes and dreams and love in their hearts will come here to die. We are grateful for your support for this project but when you are gone we will still be here living and dying. I hope you will remember that."

"What a coward," Rayna said as they walked quickly up the hill. They had exited Bailey-Boushay immediately after Ricky stopped speaking. Car and Circe had sped away from the curb after giving the two women fast, hard hugs. Circe had promised to call Rayna later in the week.

"Girl, I don't know what you're beating up on yourself for," Novel said. "Getting out of there wasn't cowardly, it was using the good sense God gave you."

"But Ricky looked so bad. What if I don't get a chance to see him again? What if he dies? I could've told him I'm sorry. Held his hand. Gave him a hug. Something. Anything other than running away."

"Well, call me a coward then. Face it, Rayna, the boy's got AIDS. You know he's going to die. You don't want to get up next to him and get anything he's got, do you? I'm just glad I didn't get anybody's number while I was there. Jesus. I knew this AIDS thing was going to bring bad luck," Novel grumbled.

Rayna stopped walking and stood silently until Novel noticed she was walking alone.

"For all of your L.A. sophistication you're sounding awfully ignorant right now. You're a mental health professional. You know better. If I ever got AIDS, I hope you wouldn't run away from me."

"Girl, you know I'd be there for you. Stop tripping behind this mess."

Rayna tuned out the rest of Novel's anxious chatter as they hurried up Madison toward Broadway.

Later that evening Rayna opened her journal and tried to write about the excitement of the Bailey-Boushay reception, the faces she had seen, her brief reunion with Circe, but the only image that would come to her mind was the sight of Ricky, rasping and angry beyond all words, an anger that could only be expressed with guttural rage.

She didn't know anyone with AIDS. She had never expected to know anyone with AIDS.

She had been afraid of Ricky. Afraid to touch him, afraid to be near him, breathing the air he breathed.

A snake's tail of shame coiled itself inside her belly. She could feel its poison sinking deep inside her bones, oozing into the core of her soul.

July 24, 1993

I am going to write Ricky a letter. I have to apologize to him, for his pain, for my stupidity. Maybe I can ask him out to lunch.

two

Dear Ricky,
I wanted to write you this letter a long time ago, but the words
kept coming out wrong. I love you. I don't want you to be sick. I
don't want you to die. I don't want any of us to die.

Love,
Rayna Sargent

Monday, as Rayna stood at the bus stop waiting for the Number 14, she remembered the stricken look on Ricky's face at Saturday's opening. Even though the day promised to be warm, she felt a slight chill. Cowardice is cold, she told herself.

How could she have walked away from him like that? Forget Novel. If she wanted to ignore Ricky's pain, fine. Novel didn't even know him. But Rayna had spent too many pleasurable evenings discussing art and politics with Ricky inside cheap restaurants to ignore him when he was obviously in need.

Rayna wanted to give herself a vicious pinch for losing touch with Ricky over the past year. He had left messages on her answering machine several times, but she had been so focused on finishing the collage and trying to get enough paintings together for her own show that she had constantly told herself she would get back to Ricky as soon as her life slowed down. How many other people had she let drift out of her life?

She hadn't even known Ricky had AIDS. They used to see each other every couple of weeks. Was she that blind, that she hadn't noticed him losing weight? Or did she just not want to see it?

Is that why he hadn't told her? Because he could see all of the *no!* in her eyes?

They had had dinner at a Thai restaurant on Pine Street a little over one year ago. Ricky had just quit his job at the Copy Mart store and they were there to celebrate.

"I knew you'd understand, Rayna," Ricky had said as they sat at the small table brushing legs with the diners beside them. He grabbed her hand and stroked it as gently as a lover. He stared at Rayna intensely with moist, dark eyes.

"With you, I don't have to pretend to feel guilty or worried about the future after quitting that shithole job. You know without asking why I did it, 'cause you've been there, baby."

Rayna snorted.

"God, Ricky. I'm the last person on earth to start questioning anybody about 'why did you quit that job when you don't have another one to replace it yet.' I've walked too many miles in those shoes."

"Ah, the things we must do for our art. By quitting this job, I'll be able to finish my masterwork soon."

"Well, you're doing better than I am. My masterwork is a long ways down the road. I don't know when I'll be able to get to that."

"I can't spend too much time on a piece because I get bored too easy. They try to say I'm a motor artist, because I produce my work so fast. They try to say my work is no good because of that. They try to dismiss me and my art, but they can't. Even in my community, I am dismissed. They don't know what to do with me. The only gay Filipinos they know dress up and wear high heels. I wouldn't know what to do with a high heel. But I am proud to be a faggot."

Rayna had been shocked to hear Ricky use that word. It sounded as harsh to her as the n-word.

"It is all right for me to say it. It is what I am."

"But it's not OK for me to say it," Rayna said. "I'm never going to say that word."

Ricky nodded. After a brief pause, he continued:

"I want to be the James Baldwin of the art world. I want to say the things that must be said with my art and not run from it. But at the same time, the work must be good. Baldwin said, 'all literature is protest but not all protest is literature.' I want my art to be a fist in the face of the world, but at the same time reveal its beauty and love."

"What did Baldwin mean by that statement?"

"I think he meant that some writing that protests inhumanity and mistreatment is not art, but is just words on a page, just spit."

"He also believed we must love white people, didn't he? Despite the error of their ways?"

"And this is why I believe he was a genius. He was right."

"But what a challenge. I have a problem with people who tell the oppressed they must love their oppressor."

"But look at the power of Gandhi. And Martin Luther King."

"Glorified victims. And I hate victimhood. It denies our humanity, the full range of our emotions. Victims can't be cruel or tyrannical or sanctimonious."

"Or sadists or ego-trippers or liars or fallen angels."

They had laughed together over the pointlessness of martyrdom, as they slowly sipped cheap wine. That was the last time she had seen Ricky until the reception. One of his paintings hung inside one of the patients' rooms at Bailey-Boushay. Rayna had recognized Ricky's work as soon as she saw the playful primary-colored naked baby boychild held lovingly in the arms of a fuchsia angel.

And she hadn't even given him a hug. She didn't even know he had AIDS. He'd never told her he was HIV positive.

What kind of friend had she been to him, that he hadn't trusted her with that information?

Rayna climbed aboard the bus. It hadn't quite filled with the Monday-morning pin-striped and linen-skirted commuters. She refused to become one of them. Although she had been working as a crisis line counselor for two years at Central Hospital's satellite mental health facility, Viewridge Mental Health Clinic, she would not allow the bureaucratic world into her heart.

"But Rayna, you'd make such a good lawyer," Circe had pleaded when Rayna decided to drop out of the University of Puget Sound Law School after only one semester.

"If I keep this up, that's exactly what I'll end up being: a good lawyer. I want to be an artist. I need to put all of my time and energy into that, not reading briefs."

"How in the hell are you going to take care of yourself as an artist? How is art going to put food on your table?"

"I'll find a way to make it. I can support myself until I get on my feet."

Circe had been terribly disappointed when Rayna had not returned to law school as she had predicted.

They had had that discussion eight years ago, two years after Rayna's divorce. Circe had not brought up the subject of law school again in all these years even though she had watched Rayna struggle and could have easily told her "I told you so" hundreds of times.

But Rayna still hadn't made the name for herself in the art world she thought she would have made by now. Several group shows, a solo show at the Whatcom County Museum, even donating paintings to community group auctions hadn't increased her sales to the point where she could give up her day job.

And forty was only five years down the road.

As she looked at the men reading the morning paper, she wondered if she had made a mistake. Maybe she should have a gray striped suit and shined shoes, a day planner, and a cellular phone in a briefcase.

What were her accoutrements of success? Paint under her fingernails, soft, well-worn khakis, lavender Birkenstocks?

"Mafungo shoes. Don't you wear those things when you

go out with me," Novel and C'Anne had often told her.

"Girl, you know you've gotta be from Seattle to be able to wear those shoes. One of the women I work with has the nerve to wear them with suits. How can you stand to have them on your feet? Don't stand up next to me with them on. You're gonna ruin my reputation. How do you ever expect to find somebody to love dressing like you own a piece of the Salvation Army?" Novel had asked.

Rayna chuckled to herself as she thought about her friends and their disdain for her lack of interest in fashion.

"Rayna, you know I love you like a sister, but you gotta do something about your wardrobe. I know you don't have a lot of disposable income, but you could invest in just one outfit that matches. You know, where the shirt matches the pants or the skirt matches the blouse or even both socks match. I know you're an artist and all, but most folks just don't get what you're trying to say with your clothes," C'Anne had said.

"I'm not trying to say anything with my clothes. I use my mouth to say what I need to say. I'm just trying to protect my body from the cold and those I don't want to see my nakedness."

"Rayna, I think I'd almost prefer to see you go naked, than keep on wearing the mismatched, outdated, old-fashioned grunge-hippie clothes you wear."

"Seattle put grunge on the map."

"But is that anything to be proud of?" C'Anne had asked.

"Madison and Boren," the bus driver growled.

Guess he didn't have his coffee yet either, Rayna thought

as she got off the bus and walked toward the brick office building of the clinic where she would spend the next eight hours patiently listening to people's emotional problems over the telephone.

Though Rayna felt she had an abundant well of compassion available for those who called the mental health clinic for help, this was going to be one of those days when she would have to dig extra deep in order to respond meaningfully to the relentless problems.

As she walked up the winding staircase to her office on the second floor, she tried to still her mind and enter into a meditative state. It would only take her fifty paces to reach the office she shared with another crisis counselor, a Catholic graduate student named Therese.

If she remained focused and calm and kept her eyes on the doorknob of that office, she might be able to pass the receptionists' desk without someone grabbing her and pressing into her hands an urgent message, some desperate person needing to be called right away, in spite of a stack of similar messages already waiting in her in-box.

At the top of the stairs Rayna caught a quick glimpse of the glistening blue waters of Puget Sound before she turned and walked down the hallway to her office.

In the center of the vestibule, where doctors and therapists received those who sought their services, in the center of the cranberry carpet thick as a porterhouse steak, stood a bronze sculpture, a woman, naked, with a cloth draped over her eyes, her head facing east. She had an air about her, a haughtiness that caught passersby off guard. Her long tapered fingers grasped a broken scale and clutched the weight to her pelvis as if the warmth of her womb could heal the brokenness of the stone.

The sculpture was called Justice and though politically incorrect, Rayna liked it. She nodded to Justice and walked past the glass-walled conference room with its vast rosewood table and high-backed leather chairs for the mucketymucks and big-shot psychiatrists whose eyes sometimes followed her down the hall.

The murmuring of support workers and the occasional laugh or groan of a doctor grew louder the closer Rayna came to the receptionists' desk. The smell of expensive cologne and leather hung in the air. Rayna could see that all of the phone lines were lit, but Marcy, the head receptionist, was fielding the calls as if she were an expert juggler.

"Feels awfully warm in here," Rayna said as she passed Marcy's desk.

"A/C's broken and the computers are down. Everybody's having a fit. Everything should be working again in the next half hour."

"Well, at least we know it's Monday," Rayna chuckled and moved on to her office, where she'd now have to pretend to be busy until the computers were working again.

"Wanna see a movie tonight?" C'Anne asked. Thank God the telephones still worked.

"No. I still have to get my stuff ready for the show next week at Sol's."

"I thought you were all ready to go. What's the holdup?"

"Just my usual procrastinating. There's something about

waiting until the last minute that gives me an extra shot of energy."

"Well, it would give me a heart attack. I don't see how you can do it."

Rayna chuckled. She tried to picture C'Anne Poinsett rushing to do anything. She just couldn't conjure it.

Where Rayna was chaos and lightning, C'Anne was a cool summer breeze. If Rayna didn't know C'Anne was raised in Seattle, just like her, she would have sworn C'Anne was raised sipping mint juleps on a porch in a land where heat clung to your skin like satin vines. Of course C'Anne never sweated.

"I don't either, really. It's a miracle the work gets done," Rayna continued.

"Are you busy today?"

"No, I just have busy work right now. The computers are still down even though they were supposed to be fixed this morning. The air conditioner's broken too, so you can imagine how hot it is with all of us cooped up in here."

"Have you seen Novel yet today?"

"Believe it or not, on a hot day like today, she's out getting coffee before she starts seeing clients."

"How she can drink coffee in this heat and with your air conditioner broken, I'll never know."

"Well, don't ask me, she's the one drinking it, I'm just sitting here trying to look busy."

"Don't you think they know you've been talking to your best friend all this time?"

"Right about now, I don't care what they know."

"Well, I still want you to call Theodore."

"Theodore?"

"You remember. The man I told you about with the hands. He's an X-ray technician here at the hospital, working on his master's degree in something or other. I told him all about you. He'd like to meet you for coffee or something. And he's right down the street from your clinic. Isn't that convenient?"

"Right, I remember. Look, I'm going to have to wait until this show is over to call him, OK? I just went to the Bailey-Boushay reception and next week, it's Sol's. When it rains, it pours, right?"

"Rayna, you're so art heavenly bound till you ain't no earthly good. Those paintings can't do a thing for you in that empty bed of yours."

"And they don't give me even half the aggravation of a relationship."

"You're just a control freak. You gotta leave that art alone sometime and get out in the world. Art isn't life."

"But art is my life, C'Anne. I wish you could remember that. My own mother doesn't hassle me about it like you do."

"I'm not hassling you, I just want you to get a life."

"I have a life, thank you. And it's working just fine. I said I'd call this guy after my show. And I will. It's not like I've been holed up somewhere and never had a relationship. I've had several disastrous ones, remember?"

"Your ex-husband was not a disaster. He was a . . ."

"Yeah, search for the right word. I couldn't think of one either, but what did I expect from a man who used to eat robins? Anybody who can live with a born-again Republican survivalist has all my sympathies."

"Carl was gorgeous."

"Carl Broussard was gorgeous. But too competitive and insecure about my art."

"There it is again. Your art. You better think about this art thing, girl. Don't get me wrong. I love your work. But is it more important than anything? Is it more important to you than me or your folks or Novel?"

Rayna didn't answer.

"OK. OK. Forget about our lifelong friendship. Forget how I saved you from kissing Joe Crum in third grade. Forget how I weaved that yarn in your hair to make a braid when you cut your hair trying to show off at school and it took your mother a week before she saw what you had done. A whole week before you got your behind whipped. Forget all that. . . ."

"C'Anne. Stop. Just stop."

"I'm just trying to show you . . ."

"I love you and appreciate you, but I gotta get off the phone."

"Don't hang up mad."

"I'm your friend, not your husband. You can tell him not to be mad, but it won't work with me."

"All right. All right. Not another word about your precious art. But you still promise to call Theodore after the show?"

"I promise."

"Well, I guess there's hope after all."

After hanging up from talking to C'Anne, Rayna decided to take a walk around the maze of hallways to Novel's office.

"Excuse me, Rayna."

Damn, Rayna thought as she turned to face Nigel Dawson, the head of the mental health division at the clinic.

"I hope you're not too busy," he said and paused as he glanced at her quickly over the tops of his half-glasses. The blue in his eyes was dark, smoky. "I need to get this crisis call handled by five today and no one else is available to make the call. Can you do it?"

Do I have any choice? Rayna thought. Dr. Nigel Dawson had never been told no a day in his life. Rayna nodded as she reached for the pink message slip in Nigel's hand. The wall clock read 4:20.

"You can drop a note in my box on your way out. I'd like to know what happened. This is regarding the Briggs case, maybe you're familiar with it?"

"No, I'm not familiar with it," Rayna said, wanting to get back to the office as quickly as possible. She hated it when someone gave her work to do right before it was time to go home.

"Well, a woman is making false accusations about one of our medical doctors at Central Hospital and this is her sister calling distraught about the situation. Encourage her to seek outside counseling. Conflict of interest, you understand. You'll probably be hearing a lot about this case in the next few weeks."

Rayna gave him a fake smile and walked away. She didn't care anything about the Briggs case or any other case. She just wanted to get out of this damn building on time.

Novel waved Rayna into a seat while talking in soft, sympathetic tones to someone Rayna presumed was a client. Dr. Jekyll and Ms. Hyde, Rayna thought as she heard Novel make professional murmuring sounds.

"How come you are such a good therapist and such a lousy friend?" Rayna asked Novel once she placed the telephone back into its receiver.

"There's two of us in here, girl. Why do you think I went into psychotherapy anyway?"

"'Cause you're a psycho?" Rayna teased.

"So I'd know when I was going crazy, that's why. What's up?"

"I was going to stop by for a little chat, but Dr. Nigel caught me in the hallway and gave me a time bomb just when I was ready to get out of here."

"Typical," Novel said sympathetically. "What's the time bomb?"

"Have you heard anything about a Briggs case?"

"Girl, close the door."

Rayna quickly went to the door and shut it.

"Nigel gave that case to you because a black woman is raising hell. And you, as a black woman, are supposed to be able to fix this. Our very own Dr. Mencken, rebel-psychiatrist-without-a-cause, was right in on the so-called therapy session where they tried to convince Latosha Briggs to have an abortion because she's HIV positive. Latosha says that after she refused, Dr. Van Horne, that Nazi ob-gyn doctor at Central, sterilized her without her consent."

"What?" Rayna stood up and couldn't stop shaking her head. "Did he do it?"

"What do you think?" Novel asked as she paced in front of her nearly floor-to-ceiling windows. "I don't know if he did it or not, but she sure believes he did. And a lot of folks are starting to believe her and get behind her on this. Naturally the administrators are about to die, but they would commit a Jim Jones mass suicide holding hands in the hospital cafeteria before they'd ever admit any wrong-doing by one of their chosen ones."

"Well, I have to go call the woman's sister now, try to calm her down and get her to get counseling somewhere else."

"Well, I'm glad it's you and not me. How are you going to calm her down? If this is true, I'd encourage her to come down here and wring Dr. Van Horne's neck my damn self."

"I thought you didn't care nothing about AIDS?"

"I thought *you* didn't care nothing about AIDS?"

"My grandmother always told me God don't like ugly. I don't care if it's AIDS, Raid, or whatever. None of these doctors have the right to sterilize anybody who doesn't want to be sterilized. And if he did it, he's gonna pay for it."

"And all I want to do is get out of here and go home."

"You're gonna get out of here but it might not be on time. I've got a depression support group tonight, so if you're still here at seven and you need a ride, give a holler."

"Thanks," Rayna said, as Novel wrapped her arms around an unsmiling Rayna and patted her back.

three

Too much talk about AIDS. First Ricky. Now Latosha Briggs. After I spoke with Latosha Briggs's sister, I was told Latosha found out she was HIV positive when she was two months pregnant. Dr. Van Horne told Latosha she had to have an abortion otherwise she would give birth to an AIDS baby. Latosha didn't want an abortion, but Dr. Van Horne had her meet with several of the hospital administrators who told her that having an AIDS baby was worse than having a child with spina bifida, like Latosha's ten-year-old son. They told her an AIDS baby would be a burden on society and it was wrong for her not to abort. Dr. Van Horne performed a second-trimester abortion. Latosha didn't get any counseling. Dr. Mencken's tainted portrait of the tortured life of an AIDS baby doesn't count as counseling, plus Latosha never gave her signed consent for the abortion or the sterilization. When Latosha went in for the induced labor, they put her in a room marked "Isolation" and left her alone still screaming for help fifteen minutes after the fetus was expelled. Later, a doctor at another hospital told Latosha she had a fifty-fifty chance of giving birth to an HIV-negative baby. Latosha tried to get pregnant again, but couldn't. Her new doctor discovered Latosha had been sterilized and would never have another child. Now that Latosha has full-blown AIDS, her sister is having to care for Latosha's son, in addition to her own three children, and is struggling with depression as a result. And the family believes that the stress of the abortion and Latosha's dealings with Dr. Van Horne are what finally propelled her into the last stages of AIDS.

Latosha's sister told me the case has been in the newspapers, because Latosha is suing the hospital for discrimination, inflicting emotional distress, negligence, and failure to obtain Latosha's written consent for both the abortion and the sterilization. I gave her referrals to counselors at other clinics since no way in hell would she get treatment from us.

I didn't have any idea this was going on. I've had a million things on my mind and until lately, AIDS wasn't one of them.

As Rayna stood at the clinic's first-floor elevator the next morning, she tried to shake the remnants of the dream she had had the night before about a baby with an oversized head who wouldn't stop crying.

The elevator door opened and Rayna smiled at the two women already standing inside. Neither of the women returned Rayna's smile. Rayna stepped to the rear.

The second-floor button was already illuminated. Rayna was too tired to climb a flight of stairs this morning.

Must be new clients, Rayna thought. She decided not to

engage the women in conversation. She knew from past experience if something went wrong with their visit, they would come looking for her. She would be a familiar, friendly black face. A woman who looked like them who they'd hope would be able to change things. As if a crisis counselor could change the behavior of neurotic mental health professionals.

Still, Rayna couldn't help but slide her eyes over the two. The tall, ivory-skinned woman with auburn-tinged shoulder-length dreadlocks wore a sleeveless cotton multicolored dress that almost reached the tops of her huaraches. Spaghetti-thin silver bracelets gleamed against her tanned arms. Rayna could smell that light musky scent popular among many of the politically active women in Seattle.

The short woman, who stood as stiff as a military cadet, wore a navy linen jacket over wide-legged navy and white print pants. She had on camel-colored Joan and David flats, the kind C'Anne liked to wear. She clutched a small straw handbag to her right side.

Rayna was glad she had been allowed to come in an hour later this morning since she had ended up staying until seven the night before talking to Latosha Briggs's sister, who thought she couldn't get counseling anywhere else.

Rayna sighed. Since the computers had not been repaired until close to the end of the day yesterday, she was bound to have stacks of work today. Now she'd have to work on her sketches during lunch. The last two paintings she wanted to complete for the show next week were not coming together as easily as she would have liked and her gallery owner, Sol Reese, wanted her to have at least two more large oils in the show.

"Be careful," C'Anne had told her on the phone last

night. "You're not a machine, you're an artist. I keep hearing desperation in your voice whenever you talk about your paintings for this show."

"But Sol says I need to produce more work so I can appeal to a wider range of collectors."

"Is everything Sol tells you the word of God? This isn't like you. You've never been one to follow behind what anybody told you to do."

"But this is my art, my livelihood. Sol's gallery is one of the better ones for new artists. She has international connections."

"You can't let a gallery or anybody else dictate the flow of your painting. You can't craft paintings on demand. You can't force the Muse to make an appearance."

"C'Anne, if I waited on the Muse, I wouldn't ever get anything done. That is what being an artist is to me. Being able to create even when I'm not lit up from the inside with inspiration."

"Well, I just don't want your creativity to dry up altogether from all this anxiety over a show."

"You know I love you, don't you?"

"Yeah, but do you ever listen to me? That's the question."

Rayna followed the two silent women out of the elevator. They walked toward the receptionists' desk, but hesitated at the Justice sculpture.

Rayna chuckled silently. She could see the look of disbelief on their faces. Rayna knew they had to be feminists. "Womanists, not feminists," Novel always reminded her. "Black women are womanists, not feminists."

Whatever the women would choose to call themselves, Rayna could see they did not approve of the sculpture. She moved on toward her office.

As she neared the receptionists' desk, she heard footsteps moving quickly behind her. She turned to see who was in such a hurry.

Just as she turned her head, she saw the short woman from the elevator open her handbag, remove a vial of red liquid, open the vial, and fling the liquid on the receptionist, her desk, her papers.

"What? What?" the receptionist sputtered as she looked disbelievingly at the two women.

"Latosha Briggs's blood is on your hands," the dreadlocked woman stated calmly, then she turned and walked toward the steps. The short woman started to follow, after she made sure the vial was empty.

"We thought we'd help you with your fear of AIDS-tainted blood," she said softly, but loud enough for Rayna and the receptionist to hear. "If one of you gets AIDS, would you still want to work for the hospital that sterilized Latosha Briggs just because she's HIV positive?"

"I don't . . . what? AIDS?" The receptionist started to cry.

"We can't do anything about Latosha Briggs. Why would you hurt us? Go after the doctors . . ." Rayna yelled, as the women quickly disappeared down the steps.

One of the clinic's managers, Dr. Kim, stepped up to the receptionists' desk.

"What in the hell is going on here?" he demanded. "Who was that?"

"It's something to do with the Briggs case."

Rayna did not want to tell on the women. She didn't believe the red liquid was blood. Unfortunately, the receptionist did and was nearing a state of hysteria.

"Calm down, Jenny. Tell me what happened," Dr. Kim said as he tried to soothe her.

Then he turned to Rayna and looked at her as if she had been the one to upset Jenny. He snapped, "Get security up here now. And go down and see if you can see where they went."

Rayna looked at the man as if he had lost his mind. Was she mistaken, or had security work just been added to her job description? She didn't think so. Still, she walked to the staircase as if she were a private detective.

As she moved quickly down the steps, she heard the sound of Jenny's unrequited sobs and attempts to soothe her coming from a myriad of voices.

She walked down to the first floor, all the while searching for the two angry women, but she was the only black woman to be seen. She headed for the clinic entrance and stepped outside into the bright light.

She still didn't see the women, so she decided to walk the perimeter of the clinic.

Several passersby turned to stare at her. Now what? she thought. Then her gaze dropped to the front of her blouse. The white cotton was streaked with the red liquid. Flecks of red were also on her left side, her left shoulder, and she also saw some over her shoulder, on her back.

"I'll be . . ." Rayna started to sputter. She didn't curse.

"Serves you right," said a voice behind her. "How can you stand to work for those fascists?"

Rayna turned to respond and found herself facing the two women. They didn't look any less angry or to be in any particular hurry to leave the area.

"Look, I can understand your being upset about what you think has happened to Latosha Briggs," Rayna said. "But you're taking it out on people who don't have anything to do with decision making at the clinic. We don't decide whether someone should have an abortion or not. The receptionist doesn't make those kinds of decisions, why take this out on her, or me?"

"Pass the buck, no one wants to accept responsibility for anything anymore," the short woman said.

"I accept responsibility for what I do, but what doctors at this clinic do is not my responsibility."

"But you benefit from their decisions. You get paid from the profits they make here. Don't you even care that your hospital is sterilizing black women without their knowledge? Doesn't that make you mad?"

"I don't know what that hospital is doing, I just work there."

"You don't believe us?" the tall one asked. "Do you think we'd be here if it wasn't true?"

"Look, I don't even know you. If what you're saying is true, of course I wouldn't like it. But blaming me for it just doesn't make any sense."

"Does it make any sense for someone to take away a woman's right to make her own decisions about having children?"

"I'm not saying that. I'm saying the way you're going about this is wrong. People aren't going to listen to you, they're just going to get mad. They've got me down here now looking for you, so security can deal with you."

"Well, they must not think too much of your loyalty to women or the race," the tall one said.

The short one snickered and piped in, "Or maybe they know you too well."

"Look, I'm not going to stand out here and argue with you. The clinic is not going to stop what it's doing just because you come in and try to scare a few people with phony blood."

"How do you know it's phony?" the tall one asked.

"What makes you so sure it's not Latosha's blood?" the short one asked.

Rayna stared at the women.

"Because even though I don't know you, I can't believe you'd throw AIDS-tainted blood on anybody for any reason."

"Well, maybe you just need a chance to get to know us better. And your whole clinic will know us by the time we're through."

"You're all going to wish you had never heard of us before long," the short one said and laughed.

Rayna thought the woman was wrong. She already wished she had never heard of them.

The tall one moved closer and spoke directly into Rayna's face.

"You're right. That wasn't real AIDS blood, but it sure got your attention. I have to face my ancestors. I don't know how you're going to be able to look yours in the face. What the hospital did to Latosha and who knows how many other black women or poor women was wrong. And it's wrong for you to try to defend the hospital.

"They sterilized Latosha just because she was HIV positive. Half of HIV-positive pregnant women can give birth to negative babies. It's a chance some women want to take. Nobody has the right to take that chance away. Not your clinic. Not your doctors.

"They would do the same thing to you if you ended up pregnant with AIDS. Would you be able to keep working for those fascists as if nothing was wrong then?"

Rayna shook her head and turned to walk away from the women.

"You can tell them this is the first they've heard from the Prejudice Posse, but it won't be the last."

Rayna looked at the women. They looked like rational, intelligent women. Well-dressed, articulate. What could make them act this crazy about something that hadn't even happened to them?

"Is this the only way you can find to make your point?" Rayna asked.

"Yeah, you could say that," the short one said. "At least we know they are thinking about how they treat women with AIDS at your hospital, more than they ever have before. And that's the best point we can make."

Both of the women laughed. Their laughter did not carry a shred of happiness, there was a sharp-edged, bitter quality radiating from the very core of that sound.

Rayna slowly walked inside the building. She turned toward the restroom, to try to scrub the red flecks out of her blouse.

For the last few weeks, all Rayna had believed she wanted was peace of mind to prepare for her art shows. Now, she was becoming increasingly confused.

The sight of Ricky, wasting away, had unnerved her more seriously than she could have imagined. She still saw the shadows in his face in her dreams. And he had been one who lived as if he loved life.

She, on the other hand, was full of so many fears and doubts that she felt she really hadn't started living yet at all.

She had always been afraid to have someone get too close to her, frightened that intimacy would lead to a suffocation of her spirit, or worse yet, strip the cloak of protection she had woven about herself and reveal her trembling, unclad self to the world. She was not ready to be that vulnerable, did not want to bring her self to the light.

She was afraid to have children, not because of what the responsibility would mean to her art, but because she was afraid to give birth to a child as crazy as her mother. Too often, she questioned her own mental stability. She thought she would die if she brought a schizophrenic child into the world.

Rayna thought about Latosha Briggs's willingness to have another baby even after she had learned the baby could get AIDS and though she already had a son with a serious illness.

"What are you so deep in thought about?"

Rayna jumped at the sound of Novel's voice.

"Girl, don't be sneaking up on folks after they've had crazy women try to douse them with blood," Rayna said.

"I heard what happened, so I came looking for you to see if you were all right."

"A couple of misguided sisters came up to the receptionists' desk and threw what they wanted us to believe to be AIDS-tainted blood on me and Jenny."

"The Prejudice Posse rides again."

"You know these women?"

"I know of them. Actually, they're an activist group that does good work in the community, but Dr. Van Horne's antics have them upset beyond belief. Otherwise, they'd be protesting in a way that wasn't so confrontational. They aren't extremists or nuts like the administration would like for us to believe."

"I am beginning to believe they're nuts without the administration telling me a thing. What right do they have to scare me and Jenny to death? We didn't perform a single procedure on Latosha Briggs. Why didn't they go after the doctors?"

"I'm sure they will. You know, Van Horne is saying he has a signed consent form."

"I don't care what Van Horne is saying. How am I ever going to be able to clear my mind enough to create three salable pieces by this weekend? I'm going to have to start working on them as soon as I get home from the office and keep working until dawn.

"I'm already feeling tired all the time and I don't want to spend any money on medical bills. Every extra penny I've got has to go toward art supplies for this show. I can't afford to get sick."

"Come on," Novel said as she placed her hands on Rayna's shoulders and gently began to massage the tension from Rayna's neck. "I'll walk you back to your office. Or, if you want to just sit and be still in my office for a while, you can. Take a few minutes and breathe, until you feel like you can go into your office and cope again."

"All right," Rayna said. "Having a therapist for a friend sure does come in handy. But you know what?"

"What?" Novel asked.

"All I want is a little peace of mind. Is that too much to ask for? Is it truly unreasonable that I don't want to care about Latosha Briggs or the Prejudice Posse or AIDS right now?"

"No, darling. It's not unreasonable, it just might not be realistic at this moment."

"That's what I was afraid you'd say," Rayna said, while Novel smiled wanly as they walked down the hall toward her office.

four

When I burst out of my mother's womb, I was an artist. I know with all of my being that that is what I am and all that I ever want to be. No matter the bills, the obscurity, the unknown road I will limp along in the dark, unaided by visible hands, I will continue to walk this road. That is what struck me deepest at the Bailey-Boushay reception. That is the knowledge that fuels my hands now as I prepare for my show at Sol's gallery. So tired. Finished pieces for the show. Tomorrow night is the reception. I need this show to work. I need for some monied man or woman to like my work. Like it enough to buy it. Like it enough to buy a lot of it.

Novel asked if I would do anything to sell my art. Steal. Lie. Sell my body and soul. I told her right about now, my answer would be yes.

*   *   *

Rayna couldn't believe she had finished the two pieces for the show. Sol had been pleased, though Rayna suspected Sol was more excited about the prospect of making money than she was about the artistic merits of Rayna's new work.

Rayna was glad she had worn the dress Circe had given her to the reception. It was fancier than anything she ever would have bought for herself. Still, she felt like a gift wrapped inside the sparkly folds of the sheer handpainted black fabric.

"Please wear something decent, Rayna. I'm not coming down there to see you look like a farm girl. This is a special event. You've been working hard for months. Enjoy it," C'Anne had said.

For once, Rayna was going to follow C'Anne's advice. She deserved to look good tonight. She felt as if everything she had been working on for the last ten years had led up to this moment. At last they would all see she had made the right choice about leaving law school.

Novel and C'Anne would be there. Circe and Car were coming. Some of the people from work.

"Now wouldn't it be nice to have that special someone sharing the sweet moment of victory with you at the reception?" Novel had teased the night before on the phone.

Rayna had hesitated a moment before she replied. She did not want to admit to anyone that she had begun to feel sharp twangs of loneliness as she put the finishing strokes on the show paintings. After working at a fevered pitch for so long, she was sure to have a prolonged spell when she wouldn't be able to pull any new creations out of her psyche to put onto canvas. What would she find to fill her time now?

"All my special someones will be there sharing it with me," Rayna had replied.

"Well, I admit I'm a freak. I'm one of those artists who doesn't like to be alone all the time. And doesn't like being broke one bit."

"You've sold out, Novel," Rayna had said. "Face it. If you can't get something for your art, then you don't do it."

"I can't imagine creating something that I can't get paid for, that's all. I'm just not capable of doing that."

"What about the love of it, the feeling you get when you make something out of nothing?"

"I do love it when I make some dollars appear in my bank account where there hadn't been any before. I love that feeling," Novel said and they both had laughed.

"Maybe you're right. My wallet sure isn't getting any fatter from all the paintings I've created out of love that didn't sell. I wish it wasn't like this."

"But it is. And the quicker you understand that, the better for your emotional health. If you're an artist, you want an audience. If you create stuff that only you like, and nobody buys, you're doing this as a hobby, not an art."

"I still disagree with you, but I know the marketplace doesn't."

"Good. My mentoring is helping you. You'll come around. Wait until you get a couple of collectors sniffing around your work. That money'll keep you in art supplies for days. You could maybe do temp work, instead of going in every day nine to five, which I know you hate."

"We'll see. Sol has been talking to some rich collector

about my work. He's supposed to come to the show. We'll see what happens, if anything."

"You've got to keep an open mind and think positive, girl. Don't let your feathers get ruffled if he says something stupid. Just look at his lips and keep smiling. Pretend his teeth are dollar signs. He doesn't have to have an ounce of intelligence, but he'll probably want to give you some advice. His advice will be as useless as a blind man turning around to look, but that's OK. It's to be expected. Just keep smiling and planning what you'll do with all that money."

Rayna mulled over the things Novel had told her. Was she selling out? Going after the dollar? She remembered how some of her fellow art students had always talked about becoming commercial with disdain. Like your work wasn't any good if it sold, if it made money. But at the same time, all of their eyes had lit up when they discussed the astro-nomical sums some of the popular commercial artists had received for their work.

Please let me be able to bite my tongue if anyone says something stupid about my new pieces, Rayna silently prayed. The thought of having to stay at the clinic as an unglorified therapist until she retired was not an appealing one.

"You look fabulous, Rayna," Sol cried as she rushed up to give Rayna a tight, quick hug. Everything about Sol was staccato. Rayna always pictured Sol as a short burst of hot energy. Red crinkly ball-of-fire hair and a thin body added to her firecracker look.

"The man I wanted you to meet is on his way. I want you to smile a lot. Don't give your opinions or your ideas about anything. Agree with his interpretations of your work. He's a millionaire, made his money with Microsoft. Just be good," Sol said, then she was off to give another artist instructions in social etiquette.

Rayna moved toward the champagne table. Later, she'd try some strawberries dipped in whipped cream, but she was too nervous to eat anything now.

She walked along the outer edge of the gallery, surveying the work of the other artists. She liked what she saw: glass and Plexiglas sculptures on pedestals, male torsos carved of natural wood, their sleek brown penises streaked with gold, brightly colored ceramic starfish, metaphysical acrylics by a Chinese filmmaker, monumental abstract oils. Rayna was in heaven. She thought her colorful acrylics fit in nicely with this group.

"Look at this, look at this. Industrial carpeting on the floor, white walls, an aluminum fan ceiling, track lighting. You've come a long way from showing your work in the college cafeteria," C'Anne said, laughing.

Rayna turned and gave her a hug.

"I'm so glad you could make it. Thanks for coming, Danny," Rayna said and grasped C'Anne's husband's hand in gratitude.

"Would you still be talking to me if I didn't?"

"No, but that's neither here nor there," Rayna said.

"You've got a nice crowd," Danny said, looking around. "You'll probably be a rich woman by the end of the night."

Rayna laughed nervously and gripped her plastic cup.

"Sol sure hopes so."

"Where is Sol? I'd like to meet her," C'Anne said.

"I'll get her. I'd like for you to meet each other too."

Rayna moved off into the crowd of people. She heard Sol's sharp bark coming from the opposite end of the room. She slowly made her way to her side.

"Ah, speak of the devil. Your ears must have been burning. I was just talking about you to Mr. Porter. Mr. Porter, meet Rayna Sargent, the artist I've been telling you about. Rayna, Mr. Porter."

Rayna shook the soft, large outstretched hand. Mr. Porter was shorter than Rayna, maybe five five, so she was surprised his hands were so large. She had expected him to be over six feet tall in order to be able to carry all that money around. Maybe that's why his hands were so big.

Millions of dollars had to be a heavy load.

"I had a question about your paintings. Let's look at them together, shall we?"

Rayna walked with Mr. Porter to her wall of paintings. She tried to remember to smile. She tried to remember to look at Mr. Porter's teeth and not listen to the words rolling past his lips, tried to see dollar signs when she looked inside his mouth. She tried to change the dry sound of his voice into the ping of a ringing cash register. Rayna saw C'Anne inside his eyes, saw Novel inside his eyes. She saw Circe and Car nodding encouragingly from his shoulders. She saw herself at sixty still answering the telephone in a small, cluttered office in the clinic. Rayna closed her eyes so she could not see and tried not to think. She tried not to defend her creations. She tried to become as dispassionate as Sol. This was not real life. These were not real people. These were brush strokes on canvas. But these tubes of color were poured from her heart. This was her heart on the canvas, her heart in this short fat man's mouth.

"Why are her hands shaped like that?"

Silently, Rayna began to count to ten before she offered a response.

"I wanted her hands to reflect the tension in her face," Rayna slowly replied. She hoped her face did not also reflect a certain tension.

"You haven't studied professionally, have you?"

Rayna gazed into Mr. Porter's smirking eyes.

"No. I've never been a professional student," she said. "But I've taken a few art classes. Mostly I'm self-taught."

"Yes. Of course," Mr. Porter nodded like a patron saint. "Tired of the life of a starving artist, eh?"

If she was starving and Mr. Porter had the last crumb of bread on earth to offer her, Rayna knew she could not take it from his portly hands.

"I would have to cut this painting in half in order to make it work with my collection in the blue room." Mr. Porter smiled and brushed his eyes quickly over Rayna's trembling body.

"Yes, I'm sure this one would work if I cut it."

"Then I guess this one won't work because it will not be cut in half," Rayna said and turned to walk away from Mr. Porter before she lost control and struck him in his fat face.

She could not believe Sol expected her to cut up what she had spent years creating. The nerve of him, the nerve of all of them. If this is what it meant to be commercial, they could have it. She was not going to be a part of them trying to humiliate her and destroy everything she had spent her life building.

"You look like you're ready to kill somebody, what happened to you?" Novel asked. Rayna had almost walked past her without seeing her.

"I don't want to talk to anyone right now. I'm furious and exhausted," Rayna said. "I'm leaving. If you see my folks will you tell them I had to leave because I wasn't feeling well? I'll explain later."

"But wait, I came all the way down here and you're going to act like this? At your opening? You gotta tell me something, or at least let me give you a ride home," Novel pleaded.

"That rich idiot wanted to cut my painting in half so it would fit in with his decor. I spent all that time on my work and he thinks I would let him cut my painting in half. For what? Money? There's not enough money in the world to get me to let that fool have anything of mine to do anything with."

"Hey, I told you, you can't listen to the words that come out of their mouths. It's a power thing for them. Don't get caught up in their power tripping. Just get paid."

Rayna pulled away from Novel.

"I can't believe you believe that, Novel. Would you let them bust one of your pieces in half with a sledgehammer just so you can get paid?"

"All right. All right, I see your point. I'll tell the folks, but call me later, OK? When you've got murder out of your mind."

Rayna quickly walked out of the gallery, her dream gallery, and went to catch a bus home.

five

Nobody but nobody better talk to me today about money. I feel mad enough to set the world on fire. Last night when I came home from the gallery I started to put all of my paint and brushes and art stuff into storage boxes.

Thought maybe the Salvation Army would want it, or maybe no one would want it. Maybe I'm a thirty-four-year-old fool. When I started to seriously try to figure out ways to enter corporate America with its glass ceilings, no concrete walls waiting, and tried to picture myself with a well-worn but tasteful leather briefcase and a pair of C'Anne black designer pumps, I laughed. I laughed and swung my arms like a windmill until I knocked all the clutter of my life from my desk.

I laughed until the only thing left to do was pick up my brush and paint.

*   *   *

Rayna sat on the bus with her eyes closed for most of the ride to work. The headache from the night before still hadn't left her. Her pulsing temples were on the verge of shattering. She willed herself not to think about the art show, the collector, or Sol.

She grumpily got off the bus at her regular stop. She ignored the bus driver's "Have a nice day," and walked stiffly down the street toward the clinic, her head throbbing with each step. An overweight bag lady brushed past her, the scent of rosewater drifted in Rayna's direction.

As she neared the clinic, she could see a small crowd gathered in front of the building. She saw a group of women holding placards: PREJUDICE POSSE RIDES AGAIN STOP RACIST STERILIZATIONS A WOMAN'S LIFE IS A HUMAN LIFE NO MORE DOCTOR ABUSE HUG SOMEONE WITH AIDS TODAY POSITIVE WOMEN FOR LIFE

Oh no, Rayna thought. Not this morning.

"No more abuse. No more lies," some of the women were chanting.

"Two four six eight. Racist docs discriminate," yelled others.

They were right in front of the door to her building. There was no way she could avoid them. The ache in her head increased. There was nothing she could do but walk through the angry chanting mass.

A sharp-cheeked woman with sunken eyes thrust out her hand to Rayna. Rayna slowed her determined stride and looked at the woman's hand.

"Are you afraid you might catch this?" the woman asked with a grimace.

"Catch what?"

"Some anger," a bright-faced woman with a pierced eye-brow said. "We're mad as hell. Do you know what's going on? Do you know about Latosha Briggs?"

Rayna groaned. Oh, how she wished she could say she had never heard of her. But of course she had. The whole office was in an uproar over Latosha Briggs. Especially since those women had thrown the fake HIV-positive blood on Jenny and herself. Rayna was still angry with the women for trying to frighten her in that way. Rayna had watched the entire staff's mounting hysteria as Jenny refused to be calmed and insisted on being taken to her doctor for tests.

They say you can't get it that way, Rayna had wanted to scream at the top of her lungs. But by that time no one would have listened. Everyone was caught up in their own AIDS hysteria.

"Yes, I know about Latosha Briggs," Rayna responded.

"What are you going to do about it?"

Were these women on crack or something? Rayna looked at the woman. She clearly expected a response.

"I'm sorry about what happened to Latosha Briggs, but I'm not planning to do anything but go to my job right now," Rayna said, and attempted to brush past the woman.

"You're sorry. You're sorry. That's it? That's all you're going to do is be sorry? Well, I hope you don't end up in the same position as Latosha, 'cause then you really will be sorry." The woman stepped aside to let Rayna pass.

"Wait a minute. Wait a minute. Let The Goddess speak." Rayna turned toward a gravelly voice.

A woman way past voluptuousness eased toward Rayna, the ends of her waist-long braids twisted with gold thread.

She wore a long kente-cloth dress. Rope sandals barely contained her wide feet. She motioned for Rayna to step away from the crowd.

"Daughter, we know you ain't no part of this mess," she whispered. "But we could sure use your help. People don't want to listen to us because they think we're too extreme. But some of us are carrying the HIV virus in our veins. We don't have time to be nice about this or try to pretty it up. Latosha is just about dead herself. We want to fight this thing with the clinic in her name and in the names of us all. We don't know who's going to be struck down next. We don't know. All we got is this moment in time, just this one moment. What else would you have us do? We got all the money in the world but we still don't got no cure for AIDS. Folks are walking around on the moon and all out in the stars but we still don't got no cure for AIDS. We can freeze people today and wake 'em up a hundred years from now but we still don't got no cure for AIDS. We lead the world in technological breakthroughs but we still don't got no cure for AIDS. Now they wanna fix women with HIV so they can't have no more babies. We got this in our blood and they wanna deny us life, and the right to keep making life. For some of us, that's all the power we want. The length of our lives has already been cut to the quick. People are afraid of us, not because of our protests or our marches or because we raise our voices to the heavens with our frustration, they're afraid of us because we represent what could happen to them. They're afraid to work with us, to sit by us, to breathe the same air we breathe. They're even afraid to touch us. Afraid to touch us in a time when we need human touch most of all.

You don't have to make love to us, just hold our hand. Tell us you know you don't understand how it feels, but you care how we feel. We ain't asking no more than that. Now maybe you can look in your heart and think of some way you can help us. Maybe it won't come to you right now, but maybe a little later on it will. Just think about it, that's all we're asking. You think you could do that for us, for your sisters?"

Rayna looked into the older woman's eyes. She felt as if she were looking into her mother's eyes, into Circe's eyes. There was a kindness there, a beauty and grace. She reached for the woman's hand.

"I'll think about it," Rayna said, softly. "But if you want help, you're going about it the wrong way. Nobody's going to have sympathy for what you're trying to do because you're getting on our nerves. Throwing blood on people and telling them it's got AIDS is wrong. Whatever you're doing is on your hands and between you and your God."

"Are your hands clean?" The woman with the pierced eyebrow stepped between Rayna and The Goddess. "And God, God. Who's God?"

Rayna stepped around the shouting woman and walked toward the clinic door.

"If you want my attention, you better talk about The Goddess. That's all I can understand. Fuck a God," the woman yelled at Rayna's retreating back.

The women continued their chanting as Rayna entered the sanctity of the building. She sighed when the heavy wooden door shut behind her.

At least my headache is gone, she thought as she stepped inside the elevator.

Rayna decided to call the guy C'Anne wanted her to meet as soon as she got to her desk. Beginning a relationship now couldn't be any more distracting than dealing with crazy collectors and Latosha Briggs and the Prejudice Posse.

six

August 21, 1993

Last night, Novel, C'Anne, and I met for one of our hen parties at Novel's house. I envy Novel and C'Anne's stability, the ease with which they live their lives. I hope I'll own a home of my own one day, a cottage like Novel's with dark wood and stained glass and a neat garden in the backyard with a brick patio for barbecues and a great old tree that I can wrap my arms around and hold.

Novel cooked Indian food: tandoori chicken, steamed cauliflower, a potato sauce and salad.

We had the kind of conversation that goes along with tasty food, full stomachs, a bottle of sparkling cider, and years of trust.

"This is new, isn't it?" Rayna asked, pointing at an ornate iron candelabra on Novel's fireplace mantel.

"Yeah, I finally found one just like the one you found at the swap meet last summer."

"If you had waited, we could've found another one a lot cheaper than what you paid for that one," Rayna said.

"Now you know, I don't have the patience to be shopping at no swap meet. If they don't sell it at Nordstrom's or the Bon, then I ain't buying."

"I know what you mean, Novel. I don't have a whole lot of patience for shopping myself. Rayna's got beaucoup patience when it comes to shopping at Goodwill or the flea markets, though. And she always finds such nice things. I'm trying to learn from her," C'Anne said.

"What I'm trying to learn from Rayna is how she is able to stay celibate for so long. That's the secret I want to learn. Girlfriend acts like she doesn't need that type of intimacy in her life," Novel said, as she crunched on a tortilla chip.

C'Anne laughed, a high-pitched tinkling sound. "Well, Novel, as a health care professional I know you are aware of how important it is to be highly selective when it comes to sexual intimacy. With AIDS and all these other diseases around that stay with you for the rest of your life, nobody can afford to take any chances."

"What do you have to worry about with your married self?" Novel asked.

"I talk to Mr. P. about AIDS all of the time. He's a powerful man and he travels a lot. I don't know who he might see during the course of his travels who might look good to him. I bought a box of rubbers and told him that I trusted him, but if something should happen and if some woman started to look like someone he wanted to know in the biblical sense, then he needed to protect himself and protect me. I gave him half of the rubbers and I kept half 'cause I don't know who might start looking good to me."

Rayna laughed.

"C'Anne, you talk that talk, but I can't even picture you with a man who wasn't Danny Poinsett. You've been with him since you were in high school and I know you ain't going nowhere."

"And neither is Danny," Novel said. "He's no fool. But how do you stay with someone for twenty years? I just can't picture myself living in the same house, sleeping in the same bed, using the same bathroom with the same person, year after year."

"I just take it day by day, Novel. That's all I can do. I'm not perfect, he's not perfect. We both know it. Plus, I feel like we have a spiritual connection that goes way back. I feel it most when we make love and the times when we're just quiet together, sitting still, maybe holding hands or lying with our arms around each other. That connection is what keeps us going. And we laugh a lot."

Rayna watched C'Anne's slender fingers brush her shoulder-length braids back from her face as she ate. Her dark skin gleamed as if it were made of blue stone that had been polished by loving hands. Where Rayna was tall and slender, C'Anne carried more weight on her medium-boned frame. She was the brick house woman the men in blues songs sang about. But C'Anne was anything but the blues.

"Enough about me. What's your favorite sexual fantasy?"

"What?" Novel asked.

"You know, the stuff you think about that gets you hot. I know I'm not the only one who has them," C'Anne said.

"But you're married, what do you need to have fantasies for? You got a live man right there in the bed with you. Now, us, we need fantasies," Novel said.

"With all of this talk about AIDS, fantasies might be the best way to go," Rayna said. "I'm thinking about giving up sex myself. I have to turn myself into some kind of investigator every time I get with somebody new. It's such a hassle."

"But a necessary one. I keep telling myself I can't afford to slip and not insist on safer sex anymore," Novel said. "But then I go and slip again."

"But you know better, Novel," Rayna said.

"We all know better, it's just so hard to always do better. It's scary thinking about the future of sex in our lives, and for me, the absence of sex in my life. I can be deep sometimes, but other times I just want somebody to get deep inside me," Novel replied.

The women's laughter swirled around them, warming them along with the wine and the candles flickering, the shadows dancing a sinuous dance on the wall.

"My sexual fantasies are ridiculous," Novel began.

"What do you mean by ridiculous?" Rayna asked.

"Well, stuff like . . . I've always wanted to know what it would feel like to have a bald head inside my vagina."

"Well, that's not ridiculous. Unusual maybe," Rayna said.

"I'd like to feel what it's like to have the head in there and the man talking inside me," Novel said.

"It would definitely give a new meaning to the phrase 'Talking Head,'" C'Anne said.

"Well, I don't know about you, but I need intelligent sex," Rayna said.

"I know what you mean. I don't want to let a dumb man inside my body," C'Anne agreed.

"I like intelligent conversation before and a little after," Rayna continued.

"I just need him to be breathing," Novel said, laughing.

"I had sex once on a subway. I'd like to try that again," Rayna said.

"How did you do that?" C'Anne asked.

"You've been holding out on us, Rayna. I'm proud of you," Novel said, nodding her head approvingly.

"Remember when I was in New York for that conference on African Art?"

Novel and C'Anne nodded.

"Well, I met this guy at the conference and we spent some time together. I went to his studio and he wanted to ride back with me on the subway to my hotel. It was late and there weren't many people on the train. It was dark and I didn't have any panties on and I sat on his lap and it was good."

"Ooooh, you're a nasty girl," Novel said. "I always knew you had it in you."

"I need to take some lessons from you, girl. I've always wanted to do it with a stranger on a train," C'Anne sighed.

"Well, I like to fantasize that I'm with a man and a woman and I'm wearing pearls," Novel said.

"Fantasies don't sound as bad when you say them out loud," Rayna said. "I had sex in the office of a church once."

"How did you do that?" C'Anne asked.

"I was dating the minister. He arranged it. That man made me scream in church. I called on every saint and sinner. And the Holy Ghost didn't have nothing to do with it."

"Spoken like a true hussyette," Novel said. "I used to fantasize about Jesus."

"Jesus seems asexual to me," Rayna said.

"No, he's gay," C'Anne said. "Someone told me they read somewhere that he's gay."

"I think of him in the same way I think about Michael Jackson when it comes to sex. Not at all," Rayna said.

"He kind of makes me think about S/M, all tied up on the cross like that," Novel said.

"Girl, you know you need to quit," C'Anne said, laughing.

"Sex had to be the last thing on his mind," Rayna said.

"Oh, I bet even Jesus slapped the monkey from time to time. He was human after all," Novel said.

"And he was a carpenter. They have such strong hands and forearms," Rayna admitted.

"But he couldn't talk dirty to you," C'Anne said.

"Well, I do like a man who knows how to talk to me in bed. And especially knows the way to talk to get me into the bed, kissing and caressing me with words, verbal foreplay. I like all of that. And penis size has nothing to do with it."

"Remember the time you were with that man with the huge penis and he didn't know what to do with it? You said you had to tell him to get up off of you," C'Anne said.

"How could I ever forget?" Novel said. "What a terrible waste of skin and muscle. All I could feel were those humongous testicles banging against me. It was awful. On the other hand, I've also had a man whose penis was so small I didn't know he had put it inside me. When I asked him when he was going to put it in, he told me, 'What do you mean? I've been working here for half an hour.'"

C'Anne chuckled, while Rayna and Novel howled.

"You know, it's a shame that except for C'Anne, all of us passionate women are going to waste," Rayna said.

"You know you're right," Novel said.

We sat around Novel's antique wooden table and analyzed the political antics of those in power, schemed up a plan to promote world peace and put an end to global starvation, as we ate into the early morning hours.

I have decided to make some changes in my life. To open myself to the bounty the universe has to offer, to be quiet more, to sit still and listen.

C'Anne hadn't lied when she told Rayna that the new man C'Anne wanted to introduce Rayna to, Theodore, had nice hands.

"Those long sensitive-looking fingers like you like. If the man wasn't an X-ray technician, I'd swear he was a masseur," C'Anne had told Rayna.

Rayna had to force herself not to stare at those hands, as she gazed into the amused eyes of Theodore Massey, who sat across the table from her inside The Dilettante, sipping a passion fruit Italian soda while she nursed a double latte.

Theodore was trying to explain the significance of Mohammed Ali to the world of boxing to Rayna, a woman who secretly believed most athletes were Neanderthals.

Rayna watched Theodore's lips move as sounds fell from

his mouth like melodic bouncing balls. She wondered if she could paint his hands so the light hit them just so, so the brown in his skin would be orange with flecks of green beneath? Could she capture the way the skin on his hands almost gleamed like snakeskin, as she painted those slim fingers caressing a masked woman's face?

"Mohammed Ali taught the media a lesson. They can't treat those men like slaves. Athletes make too much money. They're an industry unto themselves. Athletes have a right to their own private lives."

"Private lies?" Rayna slowly brought herself back into Theodore's monologue.

"Lives. Private lives," he said agitatedly.

"Oh, right. Well, they sign their lives away for all that money. I think they're all just high-priced slaves."

"But who working today isn't a high-priced slave? No. That's what they thought Mohammed Ali was, but he showed them. . . ."

Rayna's skin was hungry. It had been over eighteen months, almost two years since her limbs had been entwined with another's between soft sheets. Now the thought of having her naked legs caressed and delicate hands running over her body made her eyelids twitch.

She liked the smell of Theodore, his Lagerfeld cologne mixed with a deep muscular man smell. She liked the shape his compact body made as he sat in the chair opposite her.

They had been meeting for several months now trying to get some sense of each other. Normally, Rayna would have had The Talk with Theodore by now, but the sight of his hands, the promise of their electric sensation on her skin, and the pressure of her relentless celibacy distracted her.

* * *

Seven months ago, she had stopped seeing a man who had failed The Talk.

"I don't make love without a condom," Rayna had told him.

"I don't like using rubbers," he had said.

"You know, there's all kinds of condoms—lubricated, flavored, ribbed or smooth. You can even get some that glow in the dark. I'm willing to go condom shopping with you to help you find a type you like," she had offered.

"Where's the romance in putting on a rubber?" he had asked.

"We could make it a part of foreplay," she had responded. "But you know, I never think about romance when I'm scared about getting AIDS."

"I take good care of myself and I know I don't have AIDS," he had said.

"Have you been tested?"

"I don't need no test to tell me what I already know. I don't got it."

"But I know we've both had sex with other people, unless you're telling me that at thirty-eight years old, this would be your first time?" Rayna had asked unbelievingly.

"I haven't been intimate with that many people, have you?" he had asked defensively.

"It doesn't matter how many people we've been intimate with. When we sleep with each other, it's like we're sleeping with all of the people we've both gone to bed with. If we're together six months from now, we can both get tested, and if we're negative and monogamous and you aren't using IV drugs, then we can stop using the condoms. But until then, I can't enjoy sex when I'm worrying about a virus running wild in my body. So I won't have sex without using condoms."

"Well, I can't feel anything with a rubber on. I don't want to use 'em."

"Well, you can't feel anything when you're dead either," Rayna had told him as she finished her latte and exited the café.

Now it was time to have The Talk with Theodore. But she couldn't bring herself to say the words. His hands and the light. His lips soft on her skin. His hands on her body in the light, stroking, easing into that soft core where she had been happily alone but waiting still for a touch as gentle, as light-filled as Theodore's was bound to be.

And he looked so clean. Plus C'Anne had introduced them. C'Anne, her best friend. He had to be safe. How could a deadly virus enter a body with hands so filled with light?

August 29, 1993

I have been dating a man named Theodore. Nice mouth. Nice energy around him. We've been doing the usual. Hanging out. Dinner. Movies. Phone talk. No sex. Yet.

I think he will be an intelligent lover. He sent me a post-card of a little girl and boy holding hands. His inscription read: "The spirit is in the touch." He may be someone to talk to, to laugh with in and out of bed.

Maybe he will be a good friend. I don't want to jinx it, though, by putting too many expectations on this relationship before we even get out of the gate, as Novel says.

He's in graduate school, so he doesn't have a whole lot of time. But he tries to see me as much as he can.

That evening, Theodore and Rayna ate salmon pasta and sautéed asparagus tips from the extra-large indigo plates Rayna had recently purchased at The Chicken Soup Brigade's thrift shop. Theodore brought the wine.

"How long have you been painting?" Theodore asked as he surveyed several of Rayna's paintings on the walls.

She had kept her painting a secret until she felt she could trust him with this most intimate part of her life.

"Well, I've always dibble-dabbled. I just decided to start taking myself seriously a few years ago."

"Have you had any shows yet?"

"I've had a few pieces in group shows and one solo."

"I like the way you use color. There's a lot of passion in these women's faces."

"I'm glad you can see that. Most men react to the nudes' bodies, they don't even see the intensity of emotion in the faces."

"To be honest, I am having a reaction to the tension in those bodies," Theodore said and laughed. "It's good to see a black woman in the arts who isn't singing. Do a lot of us support your work?"

Rayna took a long sip of wine from her skinny wineglass.

"I get some support from people. Some say my art isn't black art."

"This isn't black art?"

"The skins are blue and green and purple. These women could be any race. Plus, they're not singing."

"Ah, if it's black art, then the people have to *really* be black."

"And singing," Rayna said and they both laughed.

Theodore insisted on washing dishes after they finished dinner.

"It's the least I can do," he said, smiling.

"Oh, I plan on getting paid for my services," Rayna said and Theodore burst out laughing. His laughter came from a deep place inside him and Rayna had always admired a man with depth.

While Theodore washed dishes, Rayna let down the foldout bed and lit the row of multicolored candles on the low table near the bed.

Safe with the knowledge that her diaphragm was firmly in place, Rayna loaded the CD player with the Sade, Anita Baker, Luther Vandross, and Toni Braxton CDs C'Anne had given her.

"These tunes put me flat on my back every time," C'Anne had told her. "Ask Mr. P., my legs open up like I'm being hypnotized. They'll have both of you good to go. And Rayna, don't play any of that weird shit you like to listen to. You want the man to make love to you, you don't want him to start chanting and meditating and shit."

Rayna stood next to the window that overlooked the street now slowly awakening to the coming night. She knew some of the dark spots moving down the street had pink and green hair, that the larger shapes were lovers strolling, that the erratic movements of some of the shapes were the motions of college boys jostling each other.

She didn't startle when Theodore eased behind her at the window. He traced the outline of her lips lightly with those fingers before he curved his body into hers as he bent to kiss her neck. They stood fastened at the window for some time.

Then Rayna turned to kiss him. As she closed her eyes, the color she saw was sapphire blue, then lavender-blue, then fuchsia.

She tried to kiss him deeply enough to see the color of his soul. But she would not see that until they had stripped and lay naked inside the Egyptian cotton sheets. Rayna took the thin layer of latex Theodore held in his hand like a gift and gently rolled it over his penis with her tongue. Then on and off through the night as they each opened the closed doors inside of themselves and revealed that naked place outside the body where the act of making love, the sex of the sex, would take them, only then did Rayna catch a glimpse of the color of Theodore's soul, and what she saw was a flash of vermilion red.

seven

Rayna sat on the slow-moving bus. She could almost ignore the loud-voiced young men in the back.

"She's a bitch, man. You need to drop her. She ain't all that. I wouldn't take nothin' offa her."

"Well, the bitch tried to tell me what to do but I set her straight. I ain't no punk."

"Yo man, did you see Teddy's picture? He took a picture of his dick and was showing it at school."

"You was jealous."

"Man, what I'm gone be jealous of. He ain't got nothin' on me."

Rayna wished she could make herself get up and tell them to be quiet, to respect the old people and women on the bus, to ask them if they couldn't see how they were frightening everyone with their loud talk and bravado? But when she saw a man who had to be three hundred pounds ease into a seat closer to the front, away from the threatening sound of those out-of-control teenage hormones, she decided to tune the boys out until she reached her destination. She had enough on her mind without getting into a fight with three oversized restless boys.

Last weekend as she had stretched contentedly under Theodore's soothing massage, he had hesitated and taken his strong fingers from her skin for a moment.

"You've got a funny-looking lump on your neck."

"Hmm, I've never noticed that before," Rayna said as she raised herself to a sitting position.

"Well, I'll just keep my hands on your lower anatomy," Theodore had said teasingly.

"That's fine with me," Rayna had teased back.

She wasn't worried about the lump, but she knew it was time for her annual gynecological checkup. She would make an appointment and have her doctor look at it.

"Still putting on weight, I see," Dr. Jamison teased in her gentle West Indian accent, her wavy Afro surrounding her kind face like a halo.

"Well, you've always told me I could stand to gain a few pounds."

"We're about the same height and weight now. I'm just warning you. After you get up to my size, you might be sorry."

"I'd be happy to look like you. Unfortunately, my weight is all going to my stomach, instead of places where I'd like some extra cushion."

"Remember, in some countries, a big woman is a sign of wealth. It's only in this country that we think we have to look like we're dying of malnutrition to be OK."

"Well, I'd rather carry that wealth in the bank than on my stomach."

The women laughed.

Dr. Jamison looked at the lump. She touched it lightly and frowned. "Rayna, I don't know what this lump is all about and I don't want you to fool around waiting for it to go away. I'm going to refer you to an internist to see what she thinks might be causing it."

Rayna did not worry as the internist, a cold woman who never looked directly into Rayna's eyes when she spoke, conducted all kinds of tests. She checked Rayna's stomach, sent her to get blood tests, and even did a spinal tap.

After searching without results, the internist sat Rayna down and said without looking at her, "Ms. Sargent, I have no idea what you've got. It's bizarre and I can't figure it out. I'd like to send you to an infectious disease specialist. I don't think we should let this lump sit on your neck without knowing what is causing it."

Rayna left her office walking inside a growing whirlwind of fear.

October 15, 1993

I am being probed examined poked tapped tested put upon put out My canvases sit and blankly stare at the walls The ink in my pen runs dry Questions stop in my throat My lumpy throat The pages of this journal lay empty amid all this pain, this wondering, this silence. Theodore's concern is starting to become a distraction.

At least the infectious disease specialist, Dr. Slope, could look Rayna in the eye when he spoke to her. More blood tests.

"I'm also going to test you for syphilis, just in case."

"In case of what? I don't have syphilis. What are you trying to say?"

"I'm not trying to say anything. I just want to be thorough and make sure there isn't something that we might have overlooked. I'm also going to do an ELISA test and a Western blot test to see if there might be a possible HIV virus infection. Are you familiar with HIV and AIDS?"

Rayna looked at the doctor's mouth as if his words were rolling clouds drifting her way from a great distance. HIV? AIDS? Was this nightmare ever going to end? Every time she turned around now someone was talking to her about AIDS. She was sick of it. The Briggs case, the Prejudice Posse, The Goddess and her strange sidekicks. Everybody in her face about AIDS. Now an AIDS test. She was going to have an AIDS test. This was the first time all of the talk about AIDS was about her.

"Ms. Sargent? Are you all right?"

"You tell me you're going to do an AIDS test on me and then ask me if I'm all right?"

"I also told you I was going to do a syphilis test but you got angry. I just want to check out all of the possibilities. Have you ever used IV drugs?"

"No."

"Have you had a blood transfusion in the last seven to ten years?"

"No."

"Had multiple sex partners, maybe had sex with a bisexual?"

"I'm in my mid-thirties. I have had sex in my life. I don't know what all of my partners have been doing sexually. I use condoms most of the time."

Rayna willed her mind to cease its calling forth of images of past lovers with whom she had not been safe: On her thirty-third birthday, she had been with Raymond, the bald-headed sculptor who loved to play chess, six months before Raymond she had been with Terence, the high school math teacher she had thought she was in love with, and before him, that awful period of time when she had been lonely and desperate, she had gone with that Q dog Matthew up to Vancouver B.C. for the weekend. That was three winters ago. They had had nonstop unprotected sex those three days. Rayna wanted to slap herself. To think she could have been infected then, by Matthew, a man who could barely keep up his conversation during dinner without eyeballing every woman in the restaurant. She couldn't believe her self-esteem had been so low.

"Some men may not call themselves homosexual, but they may still have sex with men. Other men may use drugs secretly and would never tell you that. If you've slept with someone who secretly sleeps with men or shoots IV drugs, you have been exposed to the risk of contracting HIV."

"And I wouldn't even know it."

"Nope. You wouldn't. So I'm taking these tests not to say anything about you personally, but because there could be an outside possibility that you have been exposed to the virus at some point during the last ten years."

"All right already. Take the tests. I can't believe how this lump could turn into something like AIDS. If I had known it was going to cause all this ruckus I never would have come in."

"But then you'd face the possibility of infecting other people without even knowing it."

"But they say ignorance is bliss. I'd prefer that bliss to this agony of dealing with tests and the possibility of finding out I have AIDS."

"But with knowledge you are forearmed. You can protect yourself and make sure you are taking care of your health."

"Will my job find out about this?"

"Your test results will be confidential. That doesn't mean that nobody will know your results. I, for one, will know. With anonymous testing, you're given a number so you have more protection of your privacy that way. You might want to think about getting anonymous testing if you don't want your results to inadvertently end up in the wrong hands."

Rayna left Dr. Slope's office in a daze. People walking past took the shapes of funhouse faces. The sounds and smells of the city—cars, horns, whistles, bells, exhaust, foods cooking, laughter, curses, tar, rubber, asphalt in the sun— Rayna didn't pay attention to any of them as she walked to the bus stop.

"Spare change for a beer?"

Rayna blindly emptied her pocket of change and poured it into the grasping grease-smeared hand.

"Have a good day."

Rayna turned and looked into the man's eyes. Whatever he saw inside her eyes made him get up and shuffle down the street in the opposite direction.

Novel had been right. They never should have participated in the Art from the Heart project. It had brought bad luck. She shouldn't have been surprised. Even her dream last night had been trying to tell her this time was coming.

In the dream, Rayna stood at the window inside a house she had never seen. She watched as a tornado made its way across the elongated terrain toward her.

"Run," her mother cried from inside the house as she twisted a red dress about her body. First she wrapped her own thin legs, then her narrow behind, flat belly and breasts, and then wound the red jersey up her outstretched arms and over her head until Rayna couldn't see her anymore.

Circe and Car stood beside Rayna at the window.

"Don't pay her no mind," Car said, pointing toward the back door. "We are safe in here."

Circe put her hand on Rayna's shoulder and started humming.

Rayna's mother moved slowly toward the window. The wind howled as if it had teeth. There was a hole in the middle of the red jersey dress where Rayna could see her mother's twisted face.

In the dream Rayna could smell her mother's tired breath. She could see her mother's empty eyes. A fist of cold air knocked a pane out of the window. Slivers of glass sparkled in the air. Rayna's mother moved toward Rayna; as she moved, she spun slowly in a circle.

Rayna thought her mother might cut her feet on the glass glittering on the floor, but she lightly stepped over it and Rayna did not see any blood. Rayna thought her mother might trip on the slippery fabric and fall on the wooden floor, but she kept moving, spinning, slowly spinning.

"Don't be afraid of me," she whispered to Rayna, her breath now turning into some sweet-smelling springlike thing. The red jersey shroud fell from her body. She reached for Rayna, tried to pull Rayna inside her grasping arms.

Rayna stepped back from her mother and screamed as the tornado moved inside the room. She reached for her mother's frail naked body too late. The tornado had her.

The phone had rung five times before Rayna escaped from the room in the dream. When she had picked up the receiver, she had been sure her mother would be on the other end of the line.

Dreaming about her mother had always been a bad sign. She did not know how she could still remember that woman's face so clearly. The last time she had seen her, Rayna had been three years old. Surely, she must be dead by now.

None of the family had seen or heard anything about her in years. When Rayna was fifteen and still lived with Circe and Car, the woman who was her mother had stolen a car and was caught driving naked down the freeway, headed for California, as she told the police. No one knew what voice she had heard. No one knew what that voice had told her to do.

Rayna sometimes looked into the eyes of the homeless women she saw on the streets of downtown Seattle, propped against the granite and concrete buildings, wearing rags, pantyhose rolled down to their swollen ankles, shoes with holes in the soles.

Rayna often looked into the eyes of these women and thought she saw her mother there. A hint of a smile, a wisp of hair brushed away from the eyes, a soft furrow between the brows.

Rayna gave them what spare change she had. She wanted these women to be warm, to be clothed and well fed. She hoped for these things for them as she hoped for these things for her mother, wherever and whoever she was.

"Don't you ever get curious about her, wonder how she's doing, want her to see how you've turned out?" Novel periodically asked during slow times in the office.

"Why do you think my feelings about her are ever going to change, Novel? She's been dead to me for years. And you know you can't rise from the dead."

"Jesus did."

"Well, we both know my mother ain't Jesus."

With all of the information Rayna knew about AIDS she still had never imagined that she could really get it. She knew something about safe sex, had been to the condom store and had dozens if not hundreds of varieties and textures and flavors of condoms inside a fishbowl beside her bed. She had been practicing safe sex for several years and had only slipped a few times. There was no way in the world she could have AIDS. How could this be happening to her?

She remembered when she was nine years old and afraid to go to sleep because she thought she might die. Someone had told her that sleeping was what it felt like when you died. Sleeping was death. She tried to stay up as late as she could and then when Circe had made her go to bed, she would lie beneath her covers and look up at the ceiling or outside into the black she could see through the crack in her curtains. She had always been surprised when she woke up and heard Car singing in the bathroom or Circe cooking breakfast in the kitchen.

But when you die you don't wake up, she would tell herself when she climbed out of bed in the morning and into bed at night.

October 29, 1993

Tomorrow I find out the results of my AIDS test. Although it is almost Halloween and jack-o'-lanterns sit on the porches of my neighbors' houses with their obscene smiles, I wish it were April Fool's Day and Dr. Slope will greet me tomorrow afternoon at the door of his office, grinning, nodding, laughing about how the lump in my throat, and now this yeast infection that I have, are all a lie, a joke, a challenge thrown my way to test my will, to test my sense of fate and faith, to see if I really do believe in miracles or madness or mistakes. And when I wake up the sun will be shining and this bracing October wind will be gone and the silver light in the trees will be a blessing surrounding me and the rain will only be rain and not these tears that won't stop seasoning my cheeks with salt. . . . I can't talk to Theodore.

When Dr. Slope called Rayna into his office, she was praying that she had herpes. Herpes would be such a blessing. She could learn how to live with herpes. Even syphilis. She could take some medication and it would go away. But AIDS?

"Well, Rayna. I'm sorry to say that you don't have syphilis, but you have been infected with the HIV virus." Dr. Slope reached across his desk for Rayna's trembling hand.

"I know this is a shock. There is a medication, AZT, you might want to think about taking. I'm going to refer you to an AIDS counselor who can help you sort through things now. I know this is a great blow and it will take a while for it to sink in. You might even want to have another test done just to make sure. My tests are pretty conclusive, but I know you will want to try anything. . . ."

Dr. Slope stopped talking and got up from the desk and rushed to Rayna's slumping body. He pulled her up from the chair and put his arms around her.

"We'll do whatever we can to fight this thing."

eight

As Rayna sat in the school chair with her right arm resting lightly on the small desktop, she began to silently recite her litany of fears:

The fear of air, the fear of bacteria, the fear of beards and beds, the fear of being afraid, the fear of being alone, the fear of being bound, the fear of being beaten, the fear of being buried alive

Thank God the smiling woman coming toward her with rubber gloves and a needle didn't have a beard, though she did have a long strip of rubber to bind Rayna's upper arm.

The fear of being dirty, of being egotistical, the fear of being scratched, being stared at, the fear of birds, the fear of blood

Rayna watched the tip of the needle pierce her skin, she marveled at the dark tears running from the green vein in her arm. She wondered what the smiling woman wondered as Rayna's blood filled the crystalline vial. Did she think

Rayna was promiscuous? Did she think Rayna used to do drugs?

The fear of cancer and cats, the fear of certain names, of childbirth and children, the fear of churches

In churches Rayna had learned to fear certain names—blasphemer fornicator demon unholy one—and books that named names. Her little black book. So hot and heavy in her hands now. A finger pointing. A book of testimony. A book of crimes. The book of naming names. Rayna's book of desire.

The fear of being confined in a house, the fear of corpses, the fear of crossing a bridge

When you come to it, right down to it, Rayna almost couldn't enter the hospital waiting room door. Almost couldn't lift her feet to mount the stairs because she didn't want to ride the elevator, didn't want to chance seeing anyone she knew. The doctor told her she had to wait six weeks until she could take the second test. The first had been positive. She was hoping there had been a mistake. That someone had made a terrible mistake.

The fear of crowds, the fear of dead bodies, the fear of deformity, of demons, of depths and dirt, the fear of disease

Rayna tried to pinpoint when this could have gotten into her body, invaded her blood and cells and tissue. She must be able to recollect the precise moment of entry, when something so evil, when something as pernicious as this, had found a home inside her.

She knew she hadn't been infected by Theodore. He'd discovered the lump too soon after they'd become lovers. It must have been Matthew, the most sexually active man in America. She didn't know what she would do if she had now infected Terence or Raymond or Theodore.

The fear of disorder, of doctors and dogs, and dreams, the fear of drugs, the fear of duration

Rayna could not even begin to imagine enduring this invasion of her body for the duration. She had seen the ravaged bodies of the men they showed on TV. Those dark spots that tattooed their faces and limbs. That slow-motion wasting away of your very self.

The fear of elevated places, and empty rooms, the fear of enclosed space, the fear of everything, the fear of eyes

What would become of Rayna's eyes? She, a painter, must have them to work. What would she see with her eyes now? What would there be to see now that this was inside her? Would it get inside her eyes?

The fear of failure, fatigue, feces, and fire, the fear of fish and floods

Rayna's body was awash now, her body had been flooded now, her body had betrayed her now, her body was not her body now, her body, her body, Rayna started to beat her body, started to pound her breast with her bandaged arm, she did not cry out, she was not loud, she would not become an enraged black woman in need of security to escort her out of the building.

She stayed in her place in the school chair. She beat her breast until the Band-Aid loosened its hold on her skin and fell to the ground. Rayna fell to the ground. Though enraged she was not loud. The nurse on duty was alarmed. "Do not call security. I repeat, do not call security," the doctor said.

The fear of flying and fog, the fear of germs, the fear of ghosts, the fear of glass, the fear of God

Inside the black hole where Rayna disappeared after having her blood drawn for her second positive HIV test, there was no God. Though she heard whispers about God, no one ever said that word aloud when she was near. It was the devastation they saw when they looked inside Rayna's eyes that silenced any talk of God or tomorrow or promise: visions of Bantustans, infants with swollen bellies, cities where flies covered fresh meat and raw sewage spilled forth like copper geysers of repressed hope.

Soon after the second positive test result, Rayna's coworkers grew increasingly disturbed. They were used to her laughing and cracking jokes and this new Rayna was moody, distant, dangerous.

At a holiday party planning meeting Rayna did not attend because she had told them to leave her the hell alone and let her do her job, Rayna's supervisor, Joy, decided to have Novel, one of the other black women working in the clinic, talk to Rayna and *make* her do something to get her back to her old self. Otherwise, if her attitude did not improve, Rayna faced the possibility of being fired.

She still had not told Theodore. She had avoided him for weeks. She had not been woman enough to even have The Talk with Theodore, how would she get the courage, the strength, to now tell him she would one day have AIDS?

December 16, 1993

It is almost Christmas. What a present the world has given me. Every day, I walk the streets as I normally walk the streets, am now able to be cordial to my coworkers. I smile. I nod my head and move my lips as I hold the telephone receiver to my mouth and try to keep from screaming.

I know I must seek counseling for this, seek some kind of help with this. Novel will be the first one I must tell. She's a therapist. She'll know how I can learn how to cope with this.

Rayna listened to the monotone voice at the other end of the telephone. She willed herself to keep the great beast of rage at bay.

Name?

Rayna Belle Sargent.

DOB?

10/14/58.

That makes you, uh, thirty-five.

I'm glad you're good at math. It makes me feel like I'm in good hands.

Huh?

Never mind.

Oh, OK. Let's see. Address?

635 Broadway Ave. E. #8.

Are you single, married, divorced?

Single.

Any children?

Rayna was silent a long while.

Hello?

No.

No?

No children.

Are you taking any medication?

Not since I stopped taking birth control pills.

Oh, why did you stop taking them?

Rayna did not respond.

OK, I'll leave that blank. Maybe you'll trust your therapist with that information.

Rayna snorted.

Any problems with alcohol or drug abuse?

No.

Have you ever had suicidal thoughts or attempted suicide?

No, what do you think I am, crazy?

Have you ever had any previous counseling?

No.

Why are you calling for counseling today?

Because I just found out I could die from AIDS tomorrow.

Rayna had braced herself for the intrusive questions she
knew they would ask. Still, the beast shifted in the pit of her

stomach once she hung up the telephone with an appointment the following afternoon to see one of Southshore Mental Health Clinic's AIDS counselors.

The telephone rang, but Rayna let the answering machine pick up the call. She had been allowing the machine to take all of her calls this past week. She knew who was calling before she heard C'Anne's pleading voice on the other end of the telephone line.

"Rayna, would you please pick up the damn phone? I know you're there. I need to talk to you. Are you OK?"

Beep.

Thankfully, Rayna's machine took the call. Rayna could barely absorb the fact that she had the virus; she didn't have the strength to help her friend cope with the shock of it.

Theodore had stopped calling weeks ago, after Rayna had insisted he leave her alone.

Rayna would talk to C'Anne when she was ready. For the rest of her life, Rayna would remember every detail of their last conversation, when Rayna had tried to gather the courage to tell C'Anne she had found out she was HIV positive.

"I found someone new to read my tarot cards. Wanna come?"

Rayna listened to the sound of C'Anne's cool-toned voice on the other end of the telephone. Practical, rational C'Anne loved to have her tarot cards read quarterly. The same C'Anne who faithfully watched CNN and believed that if Bernard Shaw's finely tuned mouth didn't comment or report on a happening, it simply hadn't happened.

"I love you and all of your contradictions," Rayna said. "I guess this means Mr. P. isn't upset anymore about those two hundred dollars' worth of phone calls to the psychic hotline?"

"All water under the bridge. I'll be over to pick you up in twenty minutes. Mr. P. is at work, so I've got the whole day free."

"Take your time. I just tried to start a new painting."

"Still working on the masked woman?"

"Yeah. And it's taking me a while to get into this latest one, so I'll be ready for a break by the time you get here."

"Mr. P. asked if this masked woman thing you're working on is some kind of S/M thing, but I just told him to get a life."

Rayna started to laugh, then stopped. It would be nice if things were as easy as telling someone to get a life and they could. Should she tell C'Anne now?

"C'Anne . . . I . . ." Rayna paused and bit her lip until she felt as if it would bleed.

"What? Is something wrong, Rayna?"

Rayna listened to the lilting sound of C'Anne's voice. There were guitar strings and mariachis in her voice. She had so much to be happy about.

"No. Nothing's wrong."

"OK. See ya."

"Yeah," Rayna said as she slowly hung up the telephone without saying a word about the HIV. Maybe it would be easier to tell C'Anne face to face.

Ever since she found out she had tested positive it seemed

as if she were living in a dream. Each step, each breath, each sweep of her arms through the air felt accentuated and unreal. Her sharp dark eyes, usually able to focus on detail, were glazed. Her lips, languid. The bustling sounds of the street outside her studio apartment in one of the most vibrant neighborhoods in the city were muted. She no longer smiled when she heard the friends and lovers walking briskly down the avenue, cracking jokes or singing as if their lungs might burst.

Rayna no longer felt safe inside the haven of her brick building with the ivy that climbed up the sides and protected the structure inside its slender green fingers. She now realized that nothing could protect her from dying, or from this disease.

If Rayna hadn't been able to keep this deadly virus out of her own body, what did it matter whether the building she lived in was safe?

At one time, she had enjoyed the northern light that made the austere apartment radiant. She had once loved the way the sunlight caused the wood to gleam on the old oak floors and her spindly antique desk. She had loved to see the shine on the gold-framed portraits of her mother Circe, and father, Amilcar, that sat proudly on the desk.

Now when she looked at the floor-to-ceiling bookshelves that lined an entire wall of the apartment, she felt nothing. What use would the library she was trying to create have for her in the grave?

Rayna stood near the easel that held the latest canvas she had been working on. The lines weren't right, the shape of the face was wrong, the eyes . . .

Rayna picked up an unopened tube of chartreuse acrylic paint and poured a small dab into a compartment in the egg carton she used for mixing her paints.

She used her fan brush to lightly spread the chartreuse over the woman's face.

There was no way on earth she was going to be able to tell anyone about this. Not Theodore. Not Novel or her parents. Not even C'Anne. Though they had been friends since third grade and had stayed best friends even after C'Anne's folks moved their family to Baltimore, Rayna still did not know how she could even fix her lips to tell C'Anne.

Cool C'Anne. Married-thirteen-years-to-the-same-man C'Anne. C'Anne who had only slept with one man in her thirty-five years and then married him. C'Anne the only black woman Rayna knew who had two graduate degrees in science. The only black woman Rayna knew who had two graduate degrees, period. And Rayna had completed her four years of college like it had been a prison sentence, and once released she had never looked back.

C'Anne and Novel had their lives in order in a way that Rayna had never been able to achieve. They were the epitome of strong black women: invincible, multifaceted shards of sparkling glass. She must follow their example. She must be tough as the drinking gourd, a well of resilience and determination. She must not break down, must not give up.

No. She could never tell C'Anne this. Most of the people she knew didn't talk about AIDS at all. Like if they didn't say the word, the disease wouldn't become real. If they talked about it, they spoke as if it were something none of them could ever get.

How could she tell them she had it?

nine

In the dream she sat at her father's knee. In the dream his hands were as big as the world. In the dream there was something running wild inside her body, inside her blood. In the dream she was frightened. Her daddy, Car, laughed his big-as-the-world laugh. Her daddy, Car, pulled her inside his big-as-the-world arms.

"Where I come from," he said, "we all got a right to the tree of life."

"You know what that is?" he asked in the dream. In the dream Rayna shook her head.

"It's a tree run smack down the middle of the world. Ain't but two branches on that tree. One branch strong enough to hold you when you step out on it. The other branch crumble when you step out on it. Crumble right beneath your feet."

In the dream Rayna nodded as if she understood. In the dream Rayna was frightened.

"You got to find your way across that tree in your life. One minute you out walking on the one branch, happy and strong as you please. Next minute, life crumbling beneath your feet. You got to walk 'em both, though. Walk them branches till you get to the jumping-off place."

"You know what that is?" he asked in the dream.

In the dream Rayna shook her head.

"The jumping-off place take you straight into eternity," he said. "Take you straight to the middle of your dreams."

Rayna awoke to a blue sky outside the window where she'd fallen asleep on the floor. She wished she could tell Car, could tell him what was happening to her body so he could take her inside his arms and hold her, rock her, love her as he had when she was a frightened child. She turned her body away from the light.

December 19, 1993

Having a difficult time writing my thoughts down now. I'm turning the same thoughts over and around until I'd just like to get out of my mind and this body.

After leaving work that day Rayna decided to splurge and take a taxi home.

"Yes?" the driver asked irritably.

Rayna hesitated. She hated to give her money to people who acted like they didn't want it. He probably had had a bad day too, she thought as she slid into the well-worn seats of the blue and white car.

"The corner of Broadway and John," she said.

The man dismissed her as he turned and pulled the thunderous car from the curb.

She watched his face as he drove. Not much older than

she was, he seemed to only be capable of scowling. Dark brows bunched together in concentration or anger, thin flesh-colored lips pulled down at the corners. Every few minutes he slapped the front seat with his right hand.

Hope he's not married, Rayna thought. Can't imagine coming home to him and his anger every night.

"Get out of the way, you goddamn idiot!" he shouted at an elderly man waiting to make a left turn. He laid his left arm on the horn. The old man was clearly startled by the loud sound.

"I'm not in that much of a hurry," Rayna said.

"They should take their licenses away at sixty," the man said, ignoring her. "It's too dangerous having them out on the road. Look at him. I bet he can't even see me. Senile old . . ."

"Honking will probably make it worse," Rayna interrupted. She could feel all of the anger she'd been trying to hold in check begin to surface in the back of her throat.

"How dare you begrudge that old man a few minutes of time to make a turn. Where are any of us going that is so goddamn important? Does anybody's life depend on us getting wherever we're going in such a damn hurry?"

For the first time since Rayna entered the taxi, the man stopped grumbling and was silent.

He's the idiot, Rayna thought. Swearing at people, honking, in a hurry to get nowhere. At least he had his life. Why did he get to live, angry at the world, and she had to die?

Rayna felt the urge to grab him by the back of his dark hair and slap him repeatedly in the face.

Then she sighed. What good would it do to slap some sense into him? She too had taken everything for granted.

Had acted as if the most trivial matter was a thing of great consequence. The way people could afford to think and act when they thought life was without end.

"You can let me out here," Rayna said, fumbling inside her small purse.

She paid the man and got out of the cab, crying. She walked slowly up the hill without seeing. She felt as if she were swimming inside a jar of paste. Could people look at her and tell she had a disease?

Rayna walked toward the Broadway Market. She decided to spend another evening watching movies until she had to go home and face the silence of her apartment.

She hadn't lost a lot of weight, didn't have any visible signs or marks of the disease, other than swollen lymph nodes. Her body felt strong, her mind felt clear, sharp.

Maybe she didn't have to tell anyone just yet. Maybe it would take years for her to develop the full-blown disease. That's what the AIDS counselor had told her when she called the AIDS hotline to try to find out as much information about AIDS as she could possibly stand to know.

The calm voice on the other end of the line had told her that many people lived HIV positive for years before they became sick. Before they became sick.

Inevitably, one day she would get sick. Very sick. Then she would die. Would it be painful?

The photographs she had seen of AIDS patients had not given her the courage and strength to fight the disease she had thought they would. She had held the slick pages of the AIDS book in her trembling hands and touched the pained faces in the photographs, trying to discover through her fingertips what those aching eyes could tell her.

The photographs had terrified her.

Is that how she would end up? Is that how she would look?

She had never been vain, but the thought of lying in a hospital bed concentration-camp thin with those awful spots all over her body had made her weep.

No, she would kill herself first. She would have to do it before she got too sick. Get someone to help her. C'Anne? No. Even though C'Anne had a background in science, she wouldn't have the stomach to help Rayna with something like this.

Novel? Novel would laugh in Rayna's face. She'd never go for something like that. Besides, she didn't believe in black people killing themselves.

"If I was on a slave ship, maybe. Just maybe, then, I'd jump overboard," she had said one day when they were talking about suicide. "Can you imagine what it must have felt like to be herded onto those ships and stacked like pieces of wood? They say in the slave castle in Ghana there's a wall where you can still see the indentations where thousands of Africans banged their heads against the wall, going crazy, hundreds of them packed into a space meant to hold dozens. No light. No air. Lying in their own urine and feces and disease. I've got a toilet in my house and a microwave oven. I've got CDs and a washing machine. Look what our people have survived. I don't want anybody talking to me about suicide today unless they've got shackles on their feet."

Theodore might help her. He certainly knew enough about the human body and he wasn't squeamish.

But that meant she'd have to tell him she had it. And she

could never do that. Look into his sweet brown eyes and tell him she may have taken him with her into the vast and terrifying land of AIDS? No, she hoped she died first.

Besides, she hadn't talked to him in weeks.

Rayna would just have to do it herself before she got too sick, before the dementia got her. No one would take her wishes seriously then. The AIDS counselor had told her she'd have to draw up a living will before she got too sick.

Living wills, AIDS counselors, T cells, macrobiotic food. How had she lived this long without them?

The black-and-white images flickered on the screen. Rayna saw the actors' lips moving but didn't hear a word said during the film. This was the only place where she could now feel a sense of peace. And she came here nightly to feel this calm that flooded her body like a hallucinogenic drug. The disease couldn't touch her here in the dark, where muted voices caressed her gently, stroking her fears, calming her.

The actors' lives went on into infinity. When one died they'd be resurrected the next night in the same film. There was no death in the movies. All was forgiven. Saints became sinners. Scorned ones, the exalted.

With the flick of her eyelids, Rayna moved from continent to bedroom to palace to shantytown. She roamed the world without a passport.

Once she left the sanctity of the theater, though, it all came back. The needle prick, the vial of blood, the call to Dr. Slope's office, her collapse inside his arms.

Her AIDS counselor had informed her she must alert all

of her lovers. She remembered the sculptor's face, the high slant of his cheekbones, the bushy arc of his eyebrows, the sighs her bed made when he crushed his two-hundred-twenty-pound naked body into hers.

And Matthew, even Matthew the cockhound, had come upon her body as if he were easing inside a musky tabernacle. There, beside their twisting limbs, below the push and pull of their tongues, inside the baptism of sweat and shivering limbs, passion swirled around them as if it were a sacred thing.

Every face and member of the men she had bedded, every musky scent, every wisp of body hair. The moans, the shouts of joy, the ache once they had gone. The pleasure, the power, the pain. All of those sensations and smells came back to Rayna with the force of an accusatory finger pointing in her face.

"No. I don't deserve this. I'm not guilty. I'm not," she'd mumble, not caring who thought she had lost her mind as she walked, cheeks wet with tears, toward home.

December 20, 1993

Ricky Adonio left a message on my machine. He lives in Bailey-Boushay now. I called to see if I could visit him.

I met Ricky at the receptionist's desk in the lobby. When I held him in my arms, his thin body felt as fragile as bird bones. We took the elevator up to the meditation room on the second floor.

We sat on the benches in the middle of the room and stared at the stained-glass window for a long time before speaking.

"Thank you for your letter," he said. "I've been sick and I hope you understand why I didn't write back."

"I have something to tell you, Ricky," I said. "I'm HIV positive too."

Ricky nodded as if he was not surprised.

"All of my friends," he said sadly. "I'm losing all of my friends."

We sat and held hands like lovers. Ricky told me about his military father, about his two brothers and his sister who is a "Filipina princess."

"I always say, my father had two macho men sons, and two princesses," he said, chuckling. "They all knew I was different. You could see it even then. Not just because I was gay, but because I used to spend hours painting in the basement. Blue, yellow, red, a big tube of white. At least I had sense enough to use primary colors. I painted my mother landscapes, beautiful landscapes she'd hang in the living room.

"Now I can't even paint the landscapes for my birdcages anymore. That's the worst thing about this virus. It takes away everything that you love. I'll think I don't have anything left to lose and then it takes something else away from me. It takes your energy, your very zest for life. You still painting?" he asked.

"Sometimes. It's harder now. I can't seem to think about anything besides the disease," I said.

"That'll pass," he said. "Then you're going to need to find something that feeds your soul to keep you going. I've been living with my T-cell count at zero for over two years. I could hide my symptoms so that most people didn't know I was sick until I started losing so much weight. I couldn't just give up and die. I kept painting until I couldn't do that anymore, then I started making birdcages and selling them to nursing homes.

"Now I'm not strong enough to build the cages anymore, but I taught someone else to make them. The old people love the birds. They might not be able to tell you their own names, but they can tell you how many baby birds are in the cages. The birds keep them connected to life in a way nothing else does.

"You're going to have to find something to keep you connected too," he said. "Or else you'll lose your mind sitting around waiting to die.

"When I started losing strength enough to make the cages, I asked God, 'Now you're going to take my birds away from me?'

"I found out about a Native American woman who works with people with HIV. She came out to my place and chanted. While she drummed, I had visions. I saw myself moving through the four stages of life. I wove what I saw into four wall hangings that I put up in my room. I get great peace from them.

"I'm sick all the time now. I try to go out and talk to the kids. Try to tell people about this disease. The talking gives me strength. Last year I found out my brother is dying. When I went to see him at the hospital, he told me he was afraid. A wife, six kids, of course he's afraid.

"I held his hand and told him to let me go first, that I'm not afraid. That way I'll be there waiting when he comes. We cried together and it was a good thing.

"You got people in your life to help you with this thing?" he asked.

I thought about C'Anne and Novel and Theodore. Car and Circe. I nodded.

"Then that's a good thing," he said, and we sat quietly gazing into the light pouring through the colored glass of the window.

part two

ten

Novel paced the mauve carpet of her small office. Her new client would arrive shortly. She wished she had a clove cigarette to smoke. The cool feel of a cigarette between her nervous fingers would soothe her, she knew. Women always appeared calm as their lips grasped and pulled on cigarettes, with those indentations in their cheeks. Cancer sticks, her good friend Marsha called them, even though she herself sometimes smoked them.

Something about this new client made Novel nervous. Last week, the woman's landlord had strongly urged her to call for an emergency mental health appointment.

Today, Novel would try to find out why. Novel's preliminary diagnosis during their brief first meeting was clinical depression. Nothing outrageous that she could detect so far. She would have the woman complete the usual tests for depression.

The woman had presented herself as intelligent, capable, no flat affect, her associations were tight. And yet, Novel suspected there was something else behind those dark almond-shaped eyes obscured by her dark-lensed Poindexter glasses.

Novel had seen a lot of black women during the eight years she had worked at Viewridge Mental Health Clinic. She was the only black therapist in a staff of sixty mental health professionals. She worked with a lot of black clients because the women came to her because she was black and a woman.

The clinic administered mental health services to the worried well, people with good health insurance, people who had problems with minor depression or conflict on their jobs or family strife. The clinic's clients were not chronically in despair, like many of the women on Aid to Dependent Children or welfare. There were no raised voices in the clinic, no one ever lost control.

Novel did not have any desire to work with mentally distressed women on ADC. After her divorce fifteen years ago, she had been not that far from welfare herself, and she did not want to be reminded of those red beans and rice days again. She did not believe that anything she could say to these women living in abject poverty would help them achieve mental health as long as the economic realities of their lives remained unchanged.

Novel stood at the nearly floor-to-ceiling window. Her gaze dropped two floors to the street below. The movement of the Capitol Hill traffic reminded her that she was alive. Earlier that morning she had spent two hours sitting in a hard-backed chair trying to appear alert during a staff meeting. In reality she had spent that time closing her mind to the ongoing political antics of the clinic head and his staff members caught up in their office intrigues.

After the meeting, Novel and a few coworkers had commiserated.

"I looked dead in his mouth and saw his lips moving so I know he was saying something. I just haven't figured out what it was yet," Novel had told Sarah, another therapist with whom she often led domestic violence support groups.

"If that's what a Harvard education does for you, I'm glad I went to Seattle U," Sarah had said, shaking her blond curls and smiling.

"Doublespeak, doctor gibberish," Linda, the only black receptionist had said, frowning. "We are in a recession and it's starting to hit us in a serious way. I don't need a medical degree to figure that out. Layoffs are next, you watch."

The women had all sighed and shook their heads. Every few years the clinic threatened staff layoffs. This year the threats would become reality since increasing numbers of the employed were fast becoming unemployed, and fewer people could afford the cost of the insurance that entitled them to services at the clinic.

"How come it's the professional staff who don't seem to get the reality that the recession is going to affect all of us, one way or another?" Sarah had asked.

"Who is better at denial than psychotherapists and psychiatrists?" Novel had asked.

They had all laughed.

Back in her office, though, Novel knew the situation at the clinic was not at all funny. As she thought about the declining balance in her checkbook, she grew even more somber. Repaying her graduate school student loans and her house mortgage took huge bites out of her paychecks. Her fondness for boutique shopping didn't help matters. Her accountant kept trying to give her advice about investing and saving money, but his words did not penetrate until he told her what she might soon owe in income taxes.

She knew she had some seniority, but as her friend Marsha had told her, "When has seniority ever helped black people?"

"You don't know what those people have in mind for you. Seniority or not."

Novel thought she could start her own private practice if worst came to worst. But she didn't have the energy to begin the research involved in setting it up. At least that's what she told herself. Just as she was telling herself she better beg, borrow, or steal some energy, the front desk buzzed her office to let her know Rayna was waiting to see her.

Novel glanced at the slow-moving gray clouds that threatened another day of rain. No wonder there are so many depressed people in Seattle, she thought.

Gray skies and grunge music.

We only get ten good days of sunshine in this city, if that. She didn't blame her friends who had moved away from the Emerald City shortly after arriving. They had moved here without fully understanding that it was the everlasting rain that helped the city stay so green.

At least the gray skies are good for business, Novel thought as she continued to wait for Rayna.

I hope this is a friendly visit, Novel thought. Her new client should be arriving here shortly.

Rayna Sargent made Novel think of the Audre Lorde poem thanking those black women who had kept their naturals. Rayna's was not one of those sculpted high-rise affairs, her hair was a soft dark halo surrounding her round face. And she had the kind of full lips Novel's ex-husband, Peter, had been so fond of.

"You know what big lips make me think about?" he'd

always say and laugh. "Ain't nothing no little-assed lips can do for me, I need some cushion in my ride."

At least he hadn't been quite as vulgar as the rappers nowadays. Before those rap songs praising the glory of large behinds were even dreamed of, let alone popular, Peter had often told Novel, "Girl, you got an ass like a racehorse," and as many racehorse asses as he'd seen, Novel knew he ought to know.

Rayna sat in her office, waiting patiently for a chance to speak with Novel. She had to tell someone she knew she had AIDS; she felt the weight of her secret might kill her otherwise. Novel was the most logical choice. And she was a therapist. Rayna knew she wasn't going to be able to keep putting C'Anne and Theodore off. She was growing weary of the lies she was telling, tired of feeling as if she were some kind of criminal because she had a disease. Automatically, she began her litany:

The fear of going to bed, the fear of graves and gravity, the fear of hair, the fear of heart disease and heat, the fear of heaven and heights, the fear of heredity, the fear of home

Her home was beginning to feel like a grave. She wouldn't let anyone come over and she didn't dare go anywhere. She hadn't picked up a paint brush in weeks. The canvas sprinkled with layers of green covering a woman's face still stood on her easel.

The fear of horses, human beings, ice and ideas, the fear of illness, of imperfection, of infection, the fear of infinity and inoculation and injections, the fear of insanity

Rayna was beginning to believe she was going insane. She was so afraid of people now, of people knowing her secret, of them knowing that this illness would infuse her blood until her body was illuminated with disease.

She refused to sleep at night. Sleeping now reminded her of death. The thought of closing her eyes terrified her. She stayed up nights watching black-and-white reruns on television and listening to her meditation tapes.

The fear of insects and itching, the fear of jealousy, justice, and knees, the fear of lakes, the fear of learning, the fear of the left side and leprosy, the fear of light

There was no justice in this. She had railed against the God of Circe and Car, railed against The Goddess of her friends. On her knees, with the night entering her apartment like an evil thing, she had railed against what would become of her body, too weary to curse the gods for what would become of her soul.

The fear of lightning, machinery, and making decisions, the fear of making false statements, the fear of so many things, the fear of marriage, meat, and men

She could not continue making false statements. She would have to make the decision to tell the truth, to everyone. Novel, C'Anne, Theodore, Circe and Car, the people at work. All of them would have to be told. She hoped Novel would be able to help her find the words to tell them.

*   *   *

"So, how are things going?" Novel asked Rayna once they were seated in the overstuffed mauve chairs in Novel's office. Novel noticed the weariness in Rayna's face.

"I haven't been feeling well," Rayna responded. She started to say more, then stopped.

"Well, it's the cold and flu time of year again, that's for sure," Novel replied, then waited. She never tried to force anyone to reveal themselves to her before they were ready and she certainly wouldn't do that to her friend. Plus, she didn't want to start sounding like a commercial for Tylenol.

"You still feeling bad, girl?"

"No. I mean I'm not snapping at everybody anymore. But I'm not there to take care of them or make them feel better either. I've got my own problems. They're just going to have to get used to that."

"Well, I don't see why they would expect you to take care of them, that's not a part of your job description. As long as you're doing your job, then they have no reason to bother you."

Rayna shook her head disgustedly. "I've never been fired from a job in my life. But I'm getting a not-so-subtle message from Joy that that's what she'd like to see happen. All because I won't be Aunt Jemima for them."

"What happened that got you in such a funk?" Novel asked. "You've been moping around, dragging your heels for weeks. And C'Anne told me you won't return her calls. I already knew you weren't returning mine. What's going on?"

Rayna stood and walked to the window. She turned and looked at Novel sitting sedately in her chair with her cup of tea. She reached for a small ceramic turtle sitting in the windowsill. She stroked its smooth shell for a moment before she spoke.

"I'm thirty-five years old and I just found out I'm going to die," she calmly began. She walked over to the chair facing Novel and sat.

"Not only am I going to die, but what I am going to die of is going to cause me to lose my friends, have people treat me like I'm a leper, and pretty much end my sex life," she continued, her voice rising.

"If someone told you your life was going to change like that, wouldn't you act a little differently? Get some kind of attitude, maybe?"

Novel slowly nodded her head, her body rigid with stunned disbelief. A thousand whys rushed toward her lips, but years of professional training stopped the many questions from bubbling forth.

"Rayna, I am here to tell you that in that situation, what my coworkers thought about me would be the least of my worries."

"I don't care anything about my job now," Rayna sadly said. "It's only important to me because of the health insurance. One day, I'm going to need a lot of very expensive medical attention."

"Is it cancer?" Novel asked tentatively. She moved her chair until her knees lay solidly against Rayna's. She felt her stomach tighten as she waited for Rayna's reply.

Novel had never dealt with death well. Both her parents had died when she was fifteen and she had never recovered from the impact of the car that had accelerated her mother and father into the other world.

"I'm HIV positive," Rayna responded, as she held the

turtle close to her face and looked into its glassy black eyes. "That's the first time I've been able to say it out loud without crying," she continued. "I cry when I think about telling my parents, but I'm not even sure they'd understand what I was saying. My father only talks about AIDS in reference to pretty boys and Circe gets a frozen look on her face whenever she has to think that I am actually having sex.

"You know I was seeing Theodore, but I can't see him anymore. I might end up killing him too. I may have already infected him. And to think that no one will ever want to touch me again makes me want to beat my head against the wall. Plus I can't have kids now. I know I never wanted to have them before, but now this robs me of my choice."

Novel was stunned and fought with all of her years of professional training not to show it. Though she had read about the increasing numbers of black women of all ages who were contracting the AIDS virus, Rayna was the first infected woman to actually sit in her office. Plus, Rayna was her friend.

They had seen each other inside Seattle Art Supply ten years ago, had gone to a café for lattes, and had been friends ever since. Novel had been there for Rayna when she divorced Carl and pledged herself to art. Novel had then promised herself to be both a therapist and an artist. Rayna had given Novel a party for her fortieth birthday five years ago that included rituals and chanting and sitting around the floor in a circle telling secrets and womanly dreams.

How could Rayna have AIDS?

Novel was one of the therapists who had avoided AIDS patients because she didn't feel emotionally equipped to handle their relentless deaths. Now, here was Rayna Sargent, a healthy-looking, young black woman, a dear friend, telling Novel she was HIV positive.

"And no one knows?" Novel asked.

"I don't know how to trust anybody with this information. I don't know how they'll react. I'm sure it would scare everybody I work with. Look at what happened to Latosha Briggs. They might try to fire me or something."

"But it's not contagious," Novel said, shifting slightly in her chair. "Surely a group of mental health professionals knows that."

"I don't know what they know, and frankly I don't care. But I don't want them treating me like a leper or trying to get rid of me. And I need my health insurance."

"And Theodore doesn't know?" Novel asked.

"I haven't been able to tell him. I just don't know how. We've only been seeing each other a short while, and I have really come to care for him."

"And you had sex with him?"

"Yes," Rayna said. "And no, we didn't always use condoms. For the last year or so, I had been insisting that whoever I slept with use condoms. But with Theodore, that went right out of the window."

"Well, you know, women are usually infected by men. Has Theodore been tested for HIV?"

"I don't know," Rayna said.

"Rayna, you have to ask him to get tested, as well as anyone else you've had sex with."

"I feel like people are going to be making all these assumptions about who I am and what I do."

"But you can't worry about what's going on in other people's minds. You can only control what's happening inside yours," Novel said.

"I feel like I'm losing my mind. All I think about is how could this happen to me? When did it happen?"

"Maybe that's how you're trying to get a feeling of control. You could also read as much information about HIV and AIDS as you can possibly stand to keep trying to feel a sense of control. That way, you'll have some idea of what to expect and you won't feel so helpless," Novel said.

"I've started reading about it and I called the AIDS Hotline and spoke with a counselor. My doctor said there are people with HIV who have lived for a long time before it turned into AIDS."

"Yes, I'm sure that's true," Novel said, more for herself than for Rayna. "The more information you have, the more choices you can make about how you're going to live the rest of your life."

"Choices? What choices? The only choices I have now are how I want to be buried," Rayna said disgustedly.

"Actually, you have a lot of them," Novel replied calmly. She reached for Rayna's hand. It was cold and damp. "The way you eat, for one example. Whether you want to continue working at this job, for another. Stress can wear down your immune system too. If this job is too stressful, you might want to make the choice to leave it. There's no sense in keeping a job that's helping you die."

Rayna laughed. "How can I worry about my job killing me and I'm already dying?"

"Is that what you really believe, Rayna?" Novel asked pointedly. "Because if you're already dying, you don't need to be in my office holding my turtle 'cause I don't hang with dead folks."

As Rayna looked at Novel, Novel felt Rayna truly saw her concern for the first time since she had come into her office. And Novel almost smiled as she realized this angry, shapely woman could be a younger, more vulnerable version of herself, trying to appear tough and grown-up.

Rayna released her hand from Novel's, stood, and gently replaced the turtle on the windowsill. By the time she returned to her seat opposite Novel in the overstuffed chair, tears had begun to trickle down both women's cheeks.

"You know, when I first got my test results back and they were positive, I just wanted to die. I didn't care anything about living with this disease. I just wanted to die. But now, I just want to live," Rayna said, as Novel rose from her chair to embrace her.

"I know, honey. I know," Novel said, as she held Rayna protectively inside her arms.

eleven

I wish I believed in Circe's God. Wish I could fall down on my knees and pray, pull from that disintegrating well of Negro spirituals, get happy, throw up my arms and run through the streets of this city with my skirt hiked above my knees, crying out in this wilderness of isolation and death.

Wish I could look into the darkness of my future standing atop the bones of the believers, the seers, those who can heal with their hands, can make my flesh whole with their tears, the comforting holy water of their tears.

I wish I could stand in the center of the world surrounded by a gospel choir in golden robes, the resolve in their faces lifting me up in the arms of their belief, their voices rising like saviors to the heavens. I wish I could turn this sorrow into a blessing. I wish when I looked inside the hollow of my spirit, a starling of hope would rise inside me fluttering for the first time up through the bitterness of my soul breaking it down into something sweet like hope like forgiveness like salvation.

I wish I could feel anything other than the emptiness I feel when I think about my spirit and ask God, why me?

Rayna hesitantly crossed the threshold of the door leading to the meeting room where the Positive Women support group was to be held. A tremor went through her body as she entered. In the soft light she could see several women already sitting around the long table.

One woman was gently stroking another woman's back. Rayna hesitated. She had told Novel she did not want to be involved in any touchy-feely group.

"Think of it more as a healing circle, or one of Circe's prayer circles, than a place where touchy-feely stuff goes on," Novel had told her. "Though I'm sure there might be some of that. Sheila believes in healing through the power of touch. A lot of women have been helped by what happens in that group and I want you to be one of them."

"I can hardly deal with what's going on in my own life. I can't take care of anybody else right now."

"Everybody's in the group to take care of themselves, girl. They won't be looking to you to do that for them. One of the reasons I'd like for you to try the group is so you won't be isolated with this disease, trying to cope on your own. You're being stretched to the limit right now and I don't want to see you snap. It can help you to talk with women who are going through the same things you are."

Reluctantly, Rayna had agreed to attend. She still hadn't told C'Anne or Circe or Car. But Novel was right. She felt as if the weight of her secret would surely dredge her an early grave.

She took a seat in a folding chair at the far end of the table. A Japanese woman with prematurely graying hair smiled at Rayna. Rayna returned her smile.

Was she at the wrong group? These women didn't look like they had AIDS. One woman looked like somebody's grandmother. Another, a dignified matron. The other brown-skinned women couldn't be much older than Rayna. One black woman with blond punk hair looked barely twenty.

Rayna's body trembled. She could feel the emotional shield she had been wearing to protect herself from the world begin to wear away.

She couldn't make herself hard any longer. She didn't want to be here. She didn't want any of them to be here. She didn't want to know their stories or feel their pain. She didn't want to see their tears. She didn't want them to see hers. Grief was such a private thing. How could she possibly share hers with strangers?

"Welcome to Positive Women. For those of you who haven't been here before, I'm Sheila, facilitator of the group. My job is to make sure we have a safe space for women to come to every week and share what's going on in their lives now that they are HIV positive."

Rayna looked into the eyes of each of the eight women sitting at the table. One of the women saw her looking and nodded reassuringly. Rayna nodded back.

"We only have a couple of ground rules," Sheila contin-ued. "We don't interrupt each other, we let each woman speak until she is finished saying what she has to say. Anyone who wants to speak will be heard here.

"We use only our first names and do not talk about anything discussed here outside of the group. We respect each other's privacy and will maintain our confidentiality. Did I leave anything out?"

"Only that we're not about gloom and doom all of the time," the Japanese woman said. "We talk about sad things, but we laugh a lot too."

"Thanks, Kiyoko. Though it's not mandatory, we do laugh sometimes. Anyway, I'd like for us to introduce ourselves and say a little something about what brought you to the group."

Sheila sat and nodded toward Kiyoko to begin the introductions.

"Hi, I'm Kiyoko. I'm a woman who has always loved sex. And I'm not ashamed of that. Even though that love is what has brought me here tonight. I'm single, childless and I teach at Seattle Central."

"You don't have to tell us any personal information that you feel may interfere with your confidentiality," Sheila said as she saw the frown on Rayna's face. "Some of what you hear may shock you. Kiyoko, for one, will never mince words. Living underground with this disease affects us all in different ways. One of the hardest things to cope with is the shame. Shame about having the disease and shame about the way we got it. Though some of us have no shame."

"I'm a slut and I don't care who knows it," Kiyoko said, laughing.

Rayna was too tense to join in the easy laughter of the women. Plus, she too had gotten HIV by having sex and she didn't think it was at all funny.

Next, a short, well-dressed Latina spoke.

"I'm Illuminata. I got this from a blood transfusion after my husband and I were in a car accident nine years ago. This was before the blood banks tested blood for HIV. My husband is positive too.

"We haven't told anybody in our families that we have it. We go to family gatherings feeling like criminals. I've been coming to the group for almost a month now. It's the only place I can go where I don't have to hide."

The grandmotherly looking woman spoke next.

"My name is Leona and I'm HIV positive."

"Remember, this ain't AA. We don't have to do no testifying," the punk-haired young black woman said.

"Right," Leona said, flustered. She took two deep breaths and continued. "As I was saying, my name is Leona and I got HIV from my boyfriend who has been off the needle for almost five years."

The red-haired woman who had been crying when Rayna entered the room spoke. Tears were not far below the surface of her words.

"My name is Margo. I've been married for thirty-five years. I got this from my husband . . ." She shook her head as tears glistened once again in her eyes. "That's all I have to say."

Leona once again began her light stroking of Margo's back. It was almost Rayna's turn to speak. Dread swirled inside her stomach and searched for a place to solidify.

Rayna glanced at the necklace lying in the center of the table on a white square of cloth. When she looked closer, she could see that what she thought was a necklace of large stones was actually a necklace of small skulls strung together like rosary beads. The skulls were the color of dried red clay. She longed to hold one in her hands, to stroke it as lightly, as calmly as Leona was now stroking Margo's back.

The next three women acted as if they had known each other a good while. They sat close together, arms touching, one rested her head on another's shoulder. Once Rayna would have liked to paint them that way, arms around each other, comforting, sisters. Now, she only waited to hear their stories.

The woman with rich dark skin spoke next.

"I'm Tango. I'm no longer having ARC symptoms. Three months ago I was hospitalized with pneumocystis pneumonia. It was terrifying. I thought it was my time to die. I was only diagnosed with HIV eighteen months ago. I could have lived longer if I hadn't waited until my T-cell count had fallen so low by the time I got tested."

"That is what is wrong with us women," Kiyoko said. "We are so busy taking care of everyone but ourselves that we say we don't have time to get sick, don't have time for all this AIDS madness and by the time we end up in the hospital too sick to take care of anybody, it's too late."

Tango nodded, then continued.

"Maybe I could've lived long enough to see my daughter graduate. I don't know what is going to become of my children. I come here to this group for the hope it gives me. I don't have to give up and die, I can fight this thing. I learn about the things I can do to help me live as long as I can because that is my priority now, to live as long and as well as I can."

"I'm Francine and I'm a dyke," the next woman began. "I wanted to be a mother. I wanted to march in the Gay Pride

Parade holding a sign that read Lesbian Mothers for Justice or something like that, you know?

"The sperm bank I used for my artificial insemination hadn't started checking their sperm for HIV. I know, I know. I could've gone to one of my homeboys and asked them for some, but you know, I didn't trust them. Anybody will tell you anything now, and I don't believe everybody who's saying they're negative really is negative. So here I sit. I got my child, and we both got HIV."

The punk-haired woman spoke next.

"You know, it's funny, as I was sitting here listening to you speak, Francine, I kept hearing my grandmother's voice. And seeing this girl back home named Portia. It's been years since I thought about Portia, with her short boy-hair and legs full of muscles and her wide-open Mississippi smile. That's what my grandmother, who we all called Miss Lee, had always called Portia's smile. A Mississippi smile.

"I thought Portia was going to grow up and be a movie star for sure. Wasn't nobody in Hope, Texas, ever going to be as pretty as Portia.

"I had had a crush on Portia since the first time I saw her black skin gleaming from all that sweat. She had cheekbones like some kind of African Indian, Miss Lee said. And she had a wide-built body like there was enough space inside for you to pull yourself up and rest a good while.

"I had never had no crush on nobody before. I took to spying on Portia whenever I saw her in town. I'd follow her into the five-and-dime and get a *True Romance* and act like I was reading it while I watched Portia over the top of the pages. I knew the color lipsticks she liked—Tempting Tangerine and

Frosted Watermelon. She liked perfumes like Lingering Lilacs and Whispering Magnolias. Fruits and flowers.

"I thought I was going to die if I didn't find a way to get Portia to notice me soon. But then I had to figure out what to do once she noticed me."

Francine snorted and shook her head violently. "I've been in that situation too many times."

The punk-haired woman smiled at her and continued:

"I decided I was going to write her a love letter. It took me a week to write it and a month to get up the nerve to actually let the postman take the letter away from my shaking hands and Miss Lee's house in his mailbag.

"'I love you and I always will. Signed Callie Lee.'

"I have never been as scared as I was the day I listened to my words come out of my grandmother's mouth. The words, my words, sounded ugly and hateful the way my grandmother said them.

"'This is an abomination,' Miss Lee said, marching around the room like a soldier for Christ. 'There will be no evil in my house. Not in this house!' she said. As she continued her march, each word left her mouth as quick and sure as a bolt of lightning from His hands.

"'Where did you get that?' I asked as I reached for the letter I had painstakingly written for Portia's eyes alone.

"Miss Lee stopped marching. She stared as if this were the first time she could really see me since I had come to live with her when I was three years old after my mother had died in childbirth.

"'You don't worry where I got this from,' she told me. 'What's done in the dark will always come out in the light. Have you gone and lost your mind, child? Don't you know that what you are talking about here with this girl ain't nothing but the Devil in you?"

"I tried to tell her that I loved Portia, but no sooner had I started to get the words out of my mouth than my grandmother took off one of her worn leather mules and started beating me with it. I fell to the ground, begging her to stop.

"'This is love,' she told me. 'I'm going to show you what love is. If I didn't love the Lord I'd let you keep on talking this foolishness. But I do love the Lord and I didn't raise you in this house to let the Devil get his hands on you like he did your mother. I'm going to beat him out of you.'

"My grandmother beat me until she couldn't raise her arm into the air anymore. The next week I was on my way here to live with my father.

"I'm sitting here tonight, thanks to my grandmother, faithful member of Prisoners of Hope Baptist Church for over forty years. Running away from her hatefulness led me straight back to myself. Along the way, though, as I ran and sometimes hid from who I was, by trying to love men when I have always been a lover of women, I picked up a souvenir that I'll have with me for the rest of my life."

Each of the women let a sigh fall from her lips. They all carried souvenirs inside their bodies that night.

"Oh, and my name is Callie."

"Let's call ourselves the Prisoners of Hope," Francine said, laughing.

"That's as good a name as any," Tango said.

The women all turned their eyes on Rayna.

Her mouth was so dry she didn't think she was going to be able to get any words out of her throat at all. She had been thinking about all of the stories she'd heard tonight.

Callie's in particular had disturbed her. C'Anne had once told Rayna that she couldn't always run away from loving people just because her mother had given her up. Rayna had ignored her for years, but tonight C'Anne's words rang inside her ears with the clarity of a sanctuary bell. Had she too been running from herself, from loving herself and who she truly was, no matter what, for all of these years?

"All I want to say is my name is Rayna and I don't know how I got this thing and I don't know who I got it from and I was a painter but that doesn't feel important to me anymore and that scares me because that was who I was, and it was everything to me." Her words rushed out of her mouth. "I knew who I was then but I don't know who I am now. I feel like my whole life is turned inside out and nothing makes sense anymore. I don't know what *is* important anymore. I've turned into this dead thing that is alive that can't sleep at night so I spend all my time after work at the movies in the dark. Then I go home and am terrified. I don't even like to lie down anymore; my apartment feels like the inside of a coffin. I can't tell anybody I have this, I can't tell anybody anything. I imagine them looking at me funny. I see them pulling away from me, from my body; I feel poisoned. My body is poisoned. I feel diseased, I feel like something that needs to be taken out into the desert and shot. But I'm too scared to do the shooting. At first I wanted to die but now I just want to live. I want to be left alone so I can live my life in peace, but how can I be alone with this thing . . . how can I be alone with this?" And to her horror, Rayna started to cry.

"You're not alone," Callie said, and the other women murmured their assent.

Sheila stood and walked to the end of the table and knelt beside Rayna's shuddering body. She placed her large arm across Rayna's shoulder.

Rayna did not shrink away from the gentleness of Sheila's touch. She remembered her third-grade teacher, Mrs. McCloud, reaching out to embrace her and how she had pulled her body back from those long thin pinkish arms.

Sometimes Circe and Car had had a difficult time comforting her with hugs or caresses when she was young. They had learned how to talk to her in hushed tones to calm her down when she was upset, or sing to her softly like Car could do to make a deer stand still.

"No, Rayna, none of us has to go through this alone. That's why we're here. So none of us ever has to feel like they're struggling with this thing alone. We are going to look at what this disease has to teach us, what it has to tell us about life."

twelve

Rayna went straight home that evening instead of stopping at the movie theater like she usually did. She didn't fix herself anything to eat because she rarely had an appetite now.

She sat in her oversized armchair near the window but didn't turn on the lamp or any other lights. She sat there in the dark with Sheila's Buddhist prayer necklace in her lap. She moved her fingers over the well-worn bone. She held a skull in her hands and willed it to speak to her.

Sheila had told them to hold the necklace when they became anxious, to squeeze the smooth skullbeads tightly inside their hands. She said to make their mark upon the bone, to take the bone inside them. She said the skulls had been blessed, as they had been blessed, that the skulls held the stories of the earth. She had told them to tell the skull-beads their deepest, most painful secrets; to hold the neck-lace when they were sitting in the dark, alone and afraid. Sheila had told them to sing to the skulls, dance with the skulls; that the skulls would never die, that their spirits would never die, but would live on forever, pieces of them inside the bone.

"Let the skull speak through you," she had said. "Tell it what you are going through."

Sheila had told her to place her hand flat over her heart and breathe, breathe deep enough for her to feel her breath going inside all of her tight, tense places, breathe deep enough to loosen and soften them, deep enough to feel a connection with the world.

Rayna sat with the necklace, watching the rise and fall of her chest with each breath. She closed her eyes and listened to the growing silence. The tumble and jangle of her thoughts slowed. For the first time in weeks, she could sit in the dark without fear.

Rayna couldn't continue to hide from her parents. She would have to tell Circe and Car, they had a right to know. She couldn't imagine not telling them. But she didn't want to look in their faces and say the words.

Those two had loved her more than her mother ever could have. And Car so proud of her no matter what she did. Even though he didn't understand the drive inside her to be an artist instead of a lawyer, his sunny face always told her she was all right with him just the same.

But the last time she had visited, she had noticed that he was getting thinner. She had always imagined him as the strongest man in the world when she was young and he would pick her up and swing her around or scold her in his baritone voice that rose from somewhere deep inside his body as if it were coming through him from the center of the earth to frighten her. Now she could see the vulnerability inside his strength.

He would not take the news well.

Rayna knew Circe would sit quietly and listen until Rayna had finished her explanation about HIV, then she'd ask a few questions and go to the library to find the understanding she wouldn't be able to get from what Rayna had told her. If she shed a tear, Rayna would never see it. Circe would save her crying for her Jesus, would share her anger and grief with the God of her parents, as she read passages from the holy book she loved to keep beside her bed for solace, within easy reach, in preparation for moments like this.

Rayna decided to call them on the telephone. She couldn't bear to witness their initial reaction in person. She hadn't spoken to them for weeks, though they both had left weekly messages on the answering machine.

"Well, well, well. So you finally decide to give us a call. You know Amilcar has been worried out of his mind. He's been over there several times, but you're never home in the evening. I left you messages at work and I gave up on leaving messages on that hateful machine."

"I know, I know. I've had a lot on my mind lately," Rayna began.

"I didn't know what to think. But Novel called to let us know you were all right and would call us. What is going on?"

Rayna could hear Car rustling in the bed next to Circe.

"I found out I have HIV," Rayna began.

"What did you say about the TV?" Circe asked.

"What does the TV got to do with anything?" Rayna heard Car mutter. They were both listening on the one receiver.

"No. I said I found out I'm HIV positive, I'm going to get AIDS," Rayna said. She held the skull tightly in her hands, rubbing her thumb over and around its smooth surface.

"Did you say . . ."

"Yeah, I said it. AIDS. I've got it."

There was silence on the line.

"Are you all right? Do you want us to come and bring you home?"

Rayna chuckled. When she was a freshman at Seattle University, living in the dormitory, away from home for the first time, she had called home, homesick. Circe had asked the same question.

"No, I mean I'm doing OK. I've been talking to AIDS counselors and Novel, you know she's a therapist, and I went to a support group tonight for women who are HIV positive. I couldn't talk to anybody at first. I still don't believe it's real, but it's starting to sink in. And I knew I had to tell you."

"Where you going, Car?" Rayna heard Circe ask. "This time of night? You better get yourself back in the bed. She said she'll be over tomorrow after work, didn't you, Rayna?" Circe said.

"You know, it might not be a bad idea if I did come over tomorrow after work."

"I don't know what to say. I don't know anything about AIDS other than Magic Johnson and I know you haven't slept with as many people as he has.

"How on earth did you get it? Are the doctors sure? You know I don't trust doctors anymore, after Robert Franklin died from cancer of the stomach after he had gone to his doctor and his doctor told him he had indigestion.

"You might need to get three or four other opinions. You know I saw on *Oprah* the way some people with AIDS get treated and it liked to make me sick. You sure you don't want to come home?"

"I'll be there tomorrow. Right after work."

"Good, I'll fix you up something special for dinner, or are you on some funny kind of diet?"

"No, anything you fix will be fine. Where did Car go?"

"Ain't no telling. He'll be here tomorrow when you get here, though. I'm gonna think about this thing and pray on it and come up with a plan to fight it."

"Bye, Mama."

"Bye, baby."

Rayna sat alone again in the dark, the skull a witness to her tears.

Long after speaking with Rayna on the telephone, Circe sat alone in the dark of her bedroom. Car had left hours before. In the forty years of their marriage, Car had never let her see his grief. She could sense it, almost smelled it in the sweat on his back the times they had tried to love themselves back from madness, back from the cliff of tears.

She did not know what to do with her grief. A child is supposed to outlive its parents. A child should lament, see to the proper burial of its parents, tend the grave and when the singer sang the song, when the words fell from her lips like grace and christened the child motherless, the child should sit in the pew with its heart breaking into waves of red splinters. All of the mourning rightfully belonged within that child's heart, not inside the parent's aged breast, not inside Car and certainly not within Circe.

Where had she stepped off the path, gone down the wrong road, missed the last step, danced to the wrong tune?

There was a weight inside her now she would never release, an unending sigh on her lips, a moan so deep within her not even the winds from her Bible could begin to cast it out.

If she opened her mouth and let a sound out now, she would never be able to keep herself from screaming.

Circe had not come to this world for this, had not left her home forty years ago in Richmond to travel to this far place to now lose her child. Her second child.

She had also lost her first child.

An unknown man had closed his hands upon her throat and beat her during a rape. One month later, after being pushed down, pushed into, pushed beyond the boundaries of her sanity, she was pregnant. Her father, a minister, had not believed her story about the rape. Her mother had found a place where she could go and lay and have hands work upon her body to remove the rapist's seed. It was then that she had vowed she would never cry out. There in the back office with the taste of iron inside her mouth, amid the smell of ether and her own blood between her legs, there in those shadows, inside a frosty darkness that stilled her womb forever, her world shrank. She was twenty-three years old and didn't venture far from her parents' house. Her mother made a decision to try to save her child.

Three months later Circe traveled to Seattle to live with her mother's sister, Betty. A week after she had arrived, she met Car. She had not described what she felt for Car as a kind of picture-house love. It was 1954 and there was so much change in the air. How could she not want to spend the rest of her life working beside a man with so much space inside him?

Car had never given her cause to cry out in misery. Circe had never come close to breaking her promise; not even when she learned she would never carry a child successfully to term, further enlarging the bounty of all that red-eyed rapist had taken from her; still she had not cried out. She had believed in her father's words, believed in the words of God. And then a woman in her church had taken her to Rayna. A child she could be a true mother to.

Now, Circe faltered. She brushed a strand of silver-white hair from her face. She ran her fingers over the black-skinned Bible she held in her hands, then pressed her fingers into its leatherlike texture, hoping to absorb its wisdom through her touch.

Uncle Sammy was the one who had told Car how to get naked and lie on the bed to talk with the dead. First you had to have a fifth of something to drink. Car was not a drinking man; he had never understood how so many people could ignore that awful taste. But now, tonight, since Rayna called, he finally understood. It wasn't the taste they were after, it was the numbing of the senses, the soft edges placed on everything real.

Someone on his job had told him about the lethal effects of tequila. Car knew he would need to get as drunk as he could possibly get before he could actually talk to the dead.

There were so many questions he wanted to ask.

Would it hurt, there at the end? Did you close your eyes and know you were taking your last breath?

Car had waited until Circe and Rayna had gone shopping at Southcenter Mall before he removed the hidden bottle of Hornitos tequila from his toolbox in the basement. The liquor was clear as water, but when Car raised the bottle to his lips to drink, it burned a trail of fire down his throat and into the core of himself.

He climbed the stairs to his bedroom and quickly stripped, leaving his T-shirt, boxer shorts, tube socks, blue jeans, and red denim shirt in a pile on the floor covering his work shoes.

Circe wouldn't like the mess he'd made, but he planned to be done by the time she returned with Rayna. He climbed, butt-naked, onto the four-poster bed he had shared with Circe for forty years.

Uncle Sammy had told him you had to be naked. The dead wouldn't talk if you had on your clothes. They wanted to be able to get close to your skin.

Car laid on his back on the bed and stared at the ceiling.

Ninety-nine talk shows on the television set and not one of them could help him with this. Women's shows, anyway. Every last one of them for women. Even Montel and Donahue. They think women the only ones that can hurt. Then what about the swelling Car had inside his gut? The tearing empty place he had no words to name?

Rayna was his only child, his only one. He didn't have any outside children. He had never had an outside woman. Circe had been plenty woman for him and she had always told him he was only half doing his job with her. She had often told him to go on out in the world and get a taste of what other women were like, but he hadn't taken her seriously.

He thought she'd been trying to cover over some of the tipping around she'd been doing, when she told him that.

He would never forget the day he'd come home from his job painting airplanes at Boeing and Rayna, who wasn't but ten years old at the time, had run out of the house talking about the police had come to the house because some man wouldn't leave Circe alone.

If there was such a thing as the worst day in his life, that was the day.

Circe crying and carrying on, talking about some man who wouldn't leave her alone and wanted her to go with him and leave Rayna and Car for good. And even if Circe always said he didn't own her, wasn't no man ever gonna own her, Car still felt like a piece of himself had twisted up and died that day.

"My mama always said she'd never tell me to say no to life," Circe had kept muttering. Car didn't want her to say no to life either, life with him, that is. But he felt glad Circe had said no to life with that other man Car had never even seen.

He never knew what was in Circe's mind. Even now, with their one child telling them she had that disease, giving him a new worst day in his life, that disease he didn't even want to wrap his lips around the letters to say its name, he still didn't know what Circe was thinking.

"I thought only the pretty boys got that," was the first thing out of his mouth when Rayna had come to the house talking about the AIDS. Circe had shot him an ugly look, so he had kept quiet.

But he still didn't understand how his Rayna could get

something he heard that mostly pretty boys, junkies, and prostitutes got.

And Rayna hadn't had a blood transfusion like Arthur Ashe.

As Car laid on the bed, he didn't know what to do with his hands. He didn't want the dead to see him holding himself, but he was lying there naked for God and everybody to see. He could just hear Circe saying didn't God or the dead care nothing about seeing his nakedness, but Car still felt uncomfortable at the thought of them looking at him.

That tequila had made his whole body feel hot as one of those fevers Rayna said she might one day get. As he lay there on the bed, his body started to feel like it was a giant wave, and his feet started to wiggle, then the wave moved to his middle, then up to his head. He laid out his arms and pressed his hands on the sides of the bed. The bed started to turn, slowly, round and round, then faster and faster.

Car didn't like roller coasters or Ferris wheels, so he started to rise up from the spinning bed, but he felt something silvery on his forehead.

A woman's touch. Something light as those Mardi Gras feathers Circe bought when they went to New Orleans five years ago. She used those feathers now to tickle him sometimes in bed.

"Are you scared, son?"

Car thought he heard his mother whispering inside his ear.

"It's all right, son. I'm here. I'm always here."

"Mama? Is that really you?"

"Yes, Amilcar. It's me."

"What you doing here, Mama?"

"You wanted to talk to me, didn't you?"

"I wanted to talk to somebody, but I didn't know it was gonna be you."

"Something is breaking your heart, son. Cracking your big old heart right in two."

Car sat up on the bed. The spinning had stopped, but the woman kept stroking his forehead with quicksilver fingers. He bent over. Yes, there was a pain pulsing inside his chest.

"You got to let yourself feel the hurting, Car. You can't keep it bottled up inside like you did when your father passed on and then me."

Car saw his daddy laying in that coffin clear as if the funeral were being held right inside his front room. The overwhelming stench of flowers sickened him. He felt as if the stiff bright blossoms might still his very breath.

His daddy had been a sharecropper, working the Georgia land, breaking the red soil as if he were opening rich dark veins at the center of the earth.

It was the never catching up that had killed him, that had planted the seed of cancer deep within his bowels.

Car had walked behind his three brothers and four sisters as they eased past the simple pine casket, almost on tiptoe, afraid to wake their sleeping father. He had not kissed his father as his great-aunts had wanted him to. It was not because his father lay in that box, eyes fixed on the ceiling and the debt-free tomorrow that had never come, but because Car had never kissed his father even when he was awake and breathing and walking around their acre of land singing as if he had been promised something that none of them would ever know.

By the time his mother died twenty years later of a can-cer in her breast, Car was a grown man and never allowed himself to cry, not even for the death of his mother.

He had loved her, though, loved her with a fierceness that frightened him, much the same way he felt frightened for Rayna now.

"You know God didn't give us a spirit of fear, Car. You couldn't protect your daughter from life. Keep loving her and help her passing to be easy. Be hope-filled and go ahead this time and cry."

Car gasped at the sudden tightening in his chest. He fell on the bed and clasped his hands as if he were praying. His mother continued to move her fingers gently on his forehead, easing the tiny, almost inaudible cries from Car's mouth.

"Why, God? Why my baby girl?" he pleaded. "Take me, instead," he cried. "Take me."

He lay on the bed and thrashed his legs. His large muscled arms felt weak and useless as he pounded them into the bed.

He felt his mother's arms around his heaving body, holding him firmly, no matter how loud he cried, no matter how much snot ran from his nose into his open mouth.

Soon, he was still. So very still. The catch in his throat began to ease, the tightness in his chest began to loosen.

He forced himself not to cry out when he felt those airy fingers on his face once more. His mother was leaving him. Again. Her caress was the touch of farewell.

"Mama," he said, wanting to beg her to stay with him, always. "Mama, thank you," he said, sniffling, as he willed his body to roll off the bed. Once on the floor, he crawled toward his pile of clothes and began putting them on.

He had to find Rayna. He had to tell Circe his mama had come. He had to tell them both it all was going to be all right. Everything would be all right.

thirteen

C'Anne wiped her soil-tinged hands on the thighs of her rolled-up overalls. She had sprinkled the last layer of compost over the freshly weeded border in her backyard. Though the January sun was shining, there wasn't much warmth in the air. She hoped she hadn't planted the last of her fall bulbs too late. When the daffodils and tulips and crocuses rose each spring, she felt as if something opened inside her too.

Thank God Danny was in Los Angeles for an engineers' convention. She had made up her mind she would have it out with Rayna this weekend. They had never gone this long without speaking and C'Anne didn't know what she had done to upset Rayna so. She had called Rayna's parents, but they hadn't heard from her either. Novel had told C'Anne to let Rayna come to her in her own time. But C'Anne was growing increasingly disturbed.

The dream she had had the night before had frightened her enough to come up with a plan to track down Rayna today.

In the dream, Rayna was lying inside a narrow white bed. There were tubes in her arms, tubes in her nose. A woman, thin as vapor, tried to stick a needle into Rayna's arm. Rayna was sleeping, but she still tried to pull her arm away.

The woman tried to stick the needle in Rayna's finger. C'Anne began to complain loudly, tried to wave the needle away and tell the thin woman Rayna really didn't need her there. She told the thin woman she would take care of Rayna.

The woman stuck the needle deep inside Rayna's heart until C'Anne began to scream. Rayna's blood flew from her chest and swirled around the room. The thin woman moved away from Rayna's bed. C'Anne tried to push Rayna's blood back inside her body.

Rayna's skin was so dry. C'Anne took a bottle of Baby Magic lotion from the drawer beside Rayna's bed. She rubbed the lotion slowly over Rayna's shoulders, into her small breasts, across her muscled stomach, and down her lean thighs. Then she massaged lotion into Rayna's ashy feet.

But Rayna would not wake up. C'Anne kept calling her name, tried shaking her thin body lying peacefully inside the rail-thin bed, but still Rayna slept.

C'Anne woke up before dawn the next morning still trying to shout Rayna awake.

January 15, 1994

Car took the news hard as I thought he would. Circe. I'll never know about Circe. We went shopping. And shopping. And shopping. We shopped as if the act of exchanging money for goods would exchange my diseased body for a healthy one. Circe jerked clothes off the rack like there was no tomorrow.

I tried to tell her what I knew about the virus, how long it might take before I got sick, most of what the AIDS counselor told me. She didn't hear a word I said. I could tell. She had that frozen-eyed look she gets on her face when she has something on her mind.

I wanted to say, listen to me, Circe, listen. You don't have that much longer to put up with me, just listen for once.

Do you think I had the nerve to say that or anything like it to Circe?

She'da struck me dead before AIDS ever got a chance to kill me.

Circe never forgave me for going through puberty. I can see it every time I look into her eyes. The unbelievably deep sense of betrayal.

This is what women meant when they said their mothers did not like them; it was the hormones and growth and all of that mouth the mothers could not forgive, could not accept coming from the little-women selves of their daughters rising like something evil inside of their homes; it was not the daughters themselves.

Sheila says I need to tell as many people as I feel comfortable telling that I've got it. I feel like I'm setting up the people that I care about most to be hit by a two-ton semi.

C'Anne is next and then maybe, just maybe, Theodore.

Wish me luck.

*   *   *

Rayna looked at the woman on the canvas. The green in her skin was begging for attention. If she just added a speck of orange she could turn it into a ruddy complexion . . .

The phone rang.

Rayna moved toward the telephone. No, she would let the answering machine pick it up. She had been having a strong urge to paint something new, an image she saw in her mind's eye that was different from anything she had ever done before.

"Rayna, is that you or do I have the wrong number? If you're there, you better pick up this goddamn phone!"

Rayna frowned. She still wasn't ready to talk to C'Anne.

"Hey, what's happening with you? I've been calling you at work, calling you at home, stopping by, and you're never home anymore and you certainly haven't been returning my calls. Are you still seeing Theodore or is it someone new? He won't talk to me about your hot thang at all."

Rayna started to pick up the phone, but her hand wouldn't reach for it.

"It's like you dropped off the face of the earth or something. If something serious is going down and you haven't even called me I'm going to be so pissed off! What's up?"

Rayna was thankful when C'Anne finally hung up the phone. She was starting to feel guilty for her weeks-long silence.

She returned to the painting. What if she removed the woman's mask? What if she painted her bare-faced and vulnerable? Her eyes, questioning?

The telephone rang again.

"Have I done or said something to offend you? Are one of your parents ill?" C'Anne's pleading voice interrupted Rayna's concentration once again. There was no mistaking her concern.

"Rayna, you're scaring me."

Click. Relieved C'Anne had once again hung up, Rayna returned to the canvas. Again, the phone rang.

Rayna moved toward the shrill bell as if she were moving through water. Hesitantly, she picked up the phone.

"Rayna Sargent, if you don't talk to me, you're dead," C'Anne yelled on the other end of the line.

"Hello?"

"Rayna, I'm so glad you picked up the phone. I've been leaving messages, but you never call me back. How are you doing?"

Rayna took a deep breath. Sheila had told them to try taking at least five deep breaths before they gave someone the news. She took two more.

Rayna released her breath.

"Fine, thanks. I have AIDS."

"What?"

"I'm HIV positive. I'm going to get AIDS. It's definite because I had two tests. I thought there might have been some kind of mistake with the first test. So I waited six weeks and took another one. I've got it."

"Rayna. No."

"Yeah, that's what I first said. I couldn't believe it either. Still can't, really. But both of my blood tests were positive."

"I don't know what to say. I honestly don't know what to say."

"I'm going to get this down on the tape recorder. A

moment of silence from C'Anne Poinsett." Rayna laughed, but C'Anne remained quiet.

"What are we going to do?"

"I don't know, C'Anne. I'm not thinking much past the moment, to tell you the truth. One day at a time and all that, you know. I go to a support group for HIV positive women and our leader recommends keeping a journal. Luckily, I've been keeping one for years. The only thing I don't like about journals, though, is that you can't scream inside the pages."

"I can't even imagine what you must be going through. If there's anything I can do to help, anything, let me know."

"I will. I'm just so sick of crying and it's hard because I feel like I'll have to take care of the people that I tell, help them deal with it, and I'm not really able to cope with it myself yet."

"Well, I am devastated by this but you know you don't have to take care of me. Focus on taking care of yourself. I'll be right over. And you let me in when you hear me buzzing, you hear me?"

"I hear."

Rayna stared at the silent receiver in her hand. If it was going to be this difficult to tell people she loved, it was going to be so easy to tell strangers. She gently returned the receiver to its cradle. It would be nice to see C'Anne, to be able to see someone without hiding, without lying.

She moved to her perch near the window and slumped into the chair. Silver fingers of light moved slowly across the gray sky. She picked up the necklace of skulls and moved it gently across her face, skullbead by skullbead. Its cool exterior soothed her. She took a long slow breath. She and the skulls breathed together as she stroked the necklace and waited for C'Anne, her lifelong friend, to come.

By the time Rayna buzzed C'Anne into her apartment, she had stopped crying and decided to be strong for her friend, even if she had to leave her body to do it.

Rayna smiled when C'Anne blew into the room with her designer exercise outfit and Avia running shoes. Her thick black-brown braids were coiled elegantly atop her head. As usual, she didn't wear any makeup, but her dark skin gleamed with good health and even better fortune. Her eyes were sharp and clear, her lips reddened naturally. No wonder Mr. P. thought she was beautiful.

"Seven years clean and sober, Rayna. It's been seven years, today."

The two women hugged fiercely.

"I know, C'Anne. I remembered," Rayna said, pointing toward the candles she had lit on the kitchen table. "So, what will it be? Sparkling cider or Market Spice Tea?"

C'Anne laughed. "I'll take the tea, I guess. Do you want me to fix it?"

Rayna shook her head. She wanted something to do with her hands, needed them to be busy while she spoke with C'Anne.

"What CD is that?"

"That's Seal. His music has been helping me cope, let me tell you. I thought I was losing it there for a while."

C'Anne sat at the table and folded her hands.

"Why didn't you want to tell me, Rayna? You know I

wouldn't let you go through anything like this alone."
C'Anne's eyes filled with tears.

Rayna's body froze at the kitchen sink. She looked at the
wall in front of her and heard C'Anne's words rolling
toward her as if they were coming from some far-off place.

"Rayna, you were there, remember? You were there for
me, nagging me, accusing me, pushing me to get help, while
even Mr. P. was still deep in denial. You were there with me
when I hit bottom, girl. When all I could see when I looked
up was bottom. There isn't anything that can happen to you
that I won't be there for you, you understand? Not anything."

The truth at the core of C'Anne's words found its way
past the layer of protection that coated Rayna's heart. She
had thought she would always need that covering of steel to
shield her from hurt. But the pain had come whether she
chose to use a shield or not. And now it welled inside her
and threatened to burst from her lips.

Rayna called forth every ounce of control she had, not to
break down in front of C'Anne, not to open her lips and say
the words, not to ball up her fists and swing them at God,
not to let the rage leave her sightless, the sorrow to eter-
nally wound her, not to let regret bind her, not to allow the
insidiousness of this disease, this plague, to turn her into
something far beyond the world of human touch.

In the end, it was not that she had lost control, not that
she had given up the crown worn by the cult of Strong
Black Women, but that she had willingly given herself over
to the kindness of her good friend's touch. Had let her
friend pick up her slumping body from the slick linoleum to
rest on her, to feel the softness of her friend's hands stroking

her forehead, the strength of her arms rocking her, cooing, murmuring, singing softly as if she were a newborn baby, while Rayna cried, cried all of the tears she had willed herself not to shed, let all of that hunger for stillness for peace for life and love to rise like a choir inside her tears, singing once and for all, the last great gospel.

fourteen

"What's the sexiest part of your body?"

Rayna stared at the woman in disbelief. Sheila had introduced this short, burly woman as Janice, a sex educator. The other women in the group also looked at Janice as if they couldn't believe what she had just said.

"The last thing I think about now is being sexy. I don't even think about sex anymore," Illuminata said with a frown.

"What right do I have to give this disease to somebody else?" Leona asked.

"Just because your boyfriend knew he had it and slept with you without telling you, Leona, doesn't mean you have to do the same thing to others," Kiyoko said. "None of the men I've slept with in the last few years have fessed up.

"In fact, most of them say they're not even going to get tested 'cause they don't want to know if they've got it."

"Well, I got tested 'cause I wanted to know. I'm in several of the high-risk groups, so I wasn't surprised when I tested positive," Janice said. "I've shot drugs, I've had sex with men, I've worked the streets without always using protection. But I'm still not giving up my right to express myself sexually."

"I know, I know. I've heard it all before," Francine said. "Sex doesn't equal death. But I didn't even get this sexually, I got it from the sperm bank."

"I tell women all the time to get sperm from one of their friends," Callie said. "At least then they'd know where it came from. It would be sperm they could trust."

"Ain't no such thing."

"She thought it was safe, just like I thought blood from the hospital was safe. How did I know after I got in that accident and needed a transfusion that the blood would be infected? How could I possibly know that?" Illuminata asked and started crying softly.

"Why do you always start that? You act like any of us could have known we were going to end up here. You're not any more innocent than us or J. Edgar Hoover," Callie said angrily. "I'm sick and tired of straight people trying to act like so-and-so is OK 'cause they got AIDS from the blood bank or their mother, but they turn their backs on those of us who got it from having sex. Where is the compassion in this country?"

"This country is so hypocritical about sex anyway. We're sex-obsessed on one hand and sexually repressed on the other," Francine said, then each of the women jumped into the conversation, quick-tongued.

"It's that Puritan thing. They like to sneak around and act like nobody's having sex, but then look at how busy Presidents Clinton and Kennedy and all of those others could get," Kiyoko said.

"Even Martin Luther King Jr. had sex, and maybe a lot of it," Janice said.

"But he didn't have sex with a man, at least as far as we know," Callie continued. "So that makes him all right. We can close our eyes to anything else he might have done. But straight people didn't even think about AIDS until Magic Johnson got it. And then . . . voilà! It was like something had just come on the scene. Like thousands of gay men hadn't even died. Like they were invisible or something. But then a big, virile, supposedly hetero man gets HIV. You saw the hard time people had with that information. Even white people on my job were walking around in shock. Then his own teammates got scared of touching him, of getting his blood or sweat or spit on them."

"Which would probably only happen if they got in the bed with him anyway or maybe that's what they do in the locker room," Kiyoko said.

"Don't you know somebody that slept with him?" Callie asked.

"Martin Luther King?"

"Magic Johnson, silly."

"No, I don't know anybody that slept with him. Though in my wilder days down in L.A., I could have easily partied with him," Kiyoko said. "He slept with thousands of women. Can you imagine how scared they must be right now?"

"Well, you can argue all you want about how the whatevers got it," Margo said angrily. "I've been married for almost forty years and I got it from my husband and I don't know if I'm ever going to get over the anger and betrayal that I feel toward that man. I knew he was selfish, but to think that he could go out and have sex without even considering what he could bring home to me makes me want to take a knife to his throat."

"When I think about how stupid all of us are about this thing I could scream," Leona said. "We think if we are married, we're not at risk. We think if we are white, we're not at risk. We think if we have a certain income level, we're not at risk. We think if we don't sleep with men, we're not at risk. We think if we're not gay or shooting drugs or don't go down on nobody, we're not at risk. We believe that if our partners are doing something sexual with someone else, they will tell us, so we're not at risk."

"That's why so many of us are sitting around in circles in chairs in rooms inside clinics just like this one. Because we convinced ourselves that we were not at risk and didn't have anything to worry about," Callie said.

"Whenever I look at someone that I could maybe have a relationship with, I ask myself, can I trust this person with my life?" Francine asked.

"But I thought I could trust my husband," Margo said. "I had no idea what a fatal thought that would turn out to be."

"Love and trust are not fatal thoughts. We can't close ourselves off to everybody and everything life has to offer because our blood is infected with this disease. Your anger is normal and healthy given the circumstances," Sheila said. "Margo, you have been betrayed. Don't be afraid to feel those feelings. Maybe one day you and your husband will go to a counselor.

"But I hate to see any of us give up on life and loving," Sheila said. "Anyway, I'm getting a little bit off track. I'm glad you were all able to express so much emotion today. You've been letting a lot of things out these past few meetings, instead of holding it all in and keeping your hurt to yourselves.

"Before we move on to Janice's presentation, I need to let you know that Tango is back in the hospital and it isn't looking too good. If anyone would like to visit her, she's at Harborview. If you don't feel up to visiting but would like to send her a note or something, I'll be going to see her after group tonight."

"But she looked so strong at our last group," Francine said.

"It takes women faster. That's what I read, anyway. By the time we find out what we've got, it's too late to fight it. We just die off," Callie said and dropped her head.

"Fortunately, you all found out about your infection in enough time to start an effective treatment program. You can live and fight this disease for a long time," Sheila said and looked each woman sitting in the semicircle firmly in the eyes.

The women sat quietly with their thoughts for several minutes.

"Well, talking about life is where I come in. Now, no one has answered my question. Before you got this disease, what was the sexiest part of your body?" Janice asked.

Leona got a sly smile on her face. "I always thought I had sexy ankles. I liked to dress them up with ankle jewelry and go bare-legged."

Callie piped in, "Ooh yeah. My legs were the sexiest part of my body. I loved it that they were long and slim and I could put on the highest heels. My favorites were my Lucite red Valentine's Day five-inch heels. I'd wear those and a short skirt to the club and drive the girls wild!"

"I was always proud of my breasts," Kiyoko said. "They were small and tight, almost boyish. Big fat breasts always repulsed me. My titties always made me feel strong."

The women laughed. Illuminata looked as if she were about to speak, then changed her mind.

"Did you want to say something?" Janice asked.

"No. No, I . . ." Illuminata reddened.

"What do you have to lose?" Callie asked.

"I always thought my pubic hair was sexy," Illuminata said, and blushed again. "It was dark and thick and bushy. Like a wild place. I loved looking at it in the mirror when I had on my crotchless panties."

"Crotchless panties?" Leona arched her eyebrows. "I just can't picture you in crotchless panties, Illuminata."

"You've got to open up that hetero mind, girl," Francine said.

"I see I've got a lot of work to do," Janice said, laughing. "Anyone else?" She looked at Rayna.

"I know it sounds corny," Rayna began. "But I always thought my hands and my mind were the sexiest parts of my body. 'Cause of the things I could think of to do with them, I guess."

"It's not corny," Sheila said. "The sexiest part of my body is my brain 'cause that's where all my intelligence is. I like the other parts of my body too when it comes to sex, but nothing can beat my brain."

"I'd like to point out something to all of you. Each of you referred to aspects of your sexuality that you enjoyed, in the past tense, almost as if that part of your life had already died. I think that's one of the tragedies of this illness. The killing off of our sexual selves. But it doesn't have to be that way," Janice said.

"But I feel like my body is contaminated and I'm dis-eased," Illuminata said.

"You are diseased, we all are diseased," Callie said, looking at Illuminata. "We can give this to other people who have sex with us. We can kill them."

"We have a disease, but if we protect ourselves and others, we don't have to kill anybody," Sheila said.

"If everybody in the world now would just assume that everybody else has the virus and practice safer sex, AIDS could be avoided," Janice said.

"But it's too late for us. We already have it," Margo said.

"You still want to protect yourself from getting infected over and over again. There's all kinds of ways for the virus to mutate. You don't want to make yourself any sicker," Sheila said.

"I get tired every time I hear somebody start talking about safe sex," Callie said. "It sounds like too much work, too much latex and too much talking and negotiating. When I want to screw, I want to screw, not negotiate Peace Talks."

"If you would just listen and open up your mind, you would probably find more ways to enjoy your sexuality than you ever thought possible. Most women just think about genital sex when they think about sex, but there's so much more that you can do. And you don't even have to touch your partner's genitalia," Sheila said.

"But I want to touch my partner's genitalia," Callie said. "I want to put my mouth there and lick her. I want to feel her wetness. That is the pleasure for me. To nibble on her and taste her. I don't want to taste no damn latex."

"You can try putting coffee that's cooled down on the latex or use whipped cream, jelly, jam, or chocolate. Experiment," Janice encouraged.

"And I like my boyfriend's sperm in my body or in my mouth," Leona said, laughing.

"It'll still be going inside your body, it'll just be going inside the bag first. Make sure you use some nonoxynol-9 on that bad boy 'cause condoms can leak or break. They come in so many textures and tastes. Try a mint or bubble-gum one. The smell of some condoms can turn me on," Janice said.

"It's your choice. Your life. You are responsible for your sexual health. If you only want to do solo sex, fine. I don't have a problem with anything you might want to do. But for those of us who enjoy a little company when we're having sex, we need to be thinking protection, and the best way to change the way we feel about barriers and latex is to make them sexy. Eroticize them as part of our sex play.

"Sex is more than penetration. There are so many different ways to be sexual. Experiment with masturbation. Do you even know how to pleasure yourself?" Janice asked.

Margo shifted uncomfortably in her seat.

"You can try some of these sex toys, play with fruit, fantasy, consensual S/M, sexually explicit stories and videos, voyeurism, sexy talk, phone sex, and on and on. You're only limited by your imagination."

There was gentle murmuring in the room as the women rose to peruse the items Janice had placed in the center of the table. Several of the women had obviously never seen many of the objects on display.

On the table lay a sex-gadget feast fit for a safe-sex-crazy love goddess: strap-on, handheld, and double dildos of various shapes, sizes, and colors, with dildo harnesses; electric and battery double-headed, G-spot and Pink Pearl vibrators; Magic Wands; nipple clamps; ben-wa balls; butt plugs; condoms with as many flavors as Baskin-Robbins; water-based lubricants; dental dams; six-inch squares of thick bubble gum; wintergreen- and vanilla-flavored latex; finger cots; and black and white latex gloves.

"So that's what they mean when they say 'no glove, no love,'" Leona murmured.

"I used to have one of these, but it didn't work as good as a microwaved zucchini," Callie said, holding a rubbery prickly-skinned black dildo in her hands.

"To think that lesbian sex has come to this," Francine said, shaking her head disgustedly.

"I'm just glad that we know we have to protect ourselves too," Callie said. "Some of us do drugs, some of us use gay men as sperm donors, some of us sleep with men and some of us even sleep with bisexual women who sleep with men. We're at risk too."

"So what is safe for us to do if we ever do decide we want to have sex?" Francine asked.

"What would be nice is if we stopped trying to expand our ideas about what is safe to do and instead expanded our ideas about what is sexual," Sheila said.

"Sheila is absolutely right. What about an erotic massage? Just the way we use touch can be erotically stimulating, but it can also be healing. Hugging is great. Bathing together. Watching each other masturbate can be another great turn-on," Janice said.

"I love watching my partner get off," Callie said.

"Dry humping," Janice continued.

"Dry humping?" Margo asked.

"Rubbing against each other with your clothes on," Leona said. "You remember, like we did back in high school."

"You can try acting out fantasies, or just fantasizing."

"I have to admit I have had a vision of my bus driver lying bound and helpless in my bed," Illuminata said, giggling.

"Nata, I can't picture you in an S/M scene."

"How come everybody has a problem seeing me sexy?"

"I can see you in a hot little Catholic schoolgirl uniform," Callie said.

Sheila laughed. "All of this talk about safe sex must be working. When we first got here you didn't want to think about sex and now you can't stop talking about it."

"I like this better," Rayna said. "My mother always tells me to say yes to life. This feels so much better than all the nos I've been telling myself."

"That was my point. If just one of you women got that message today, then I've done what I was here to do. There's no reason why healthy sex has to be lonely or dull," Janice said. "We have a disease—"

"But we still have live puss—" Callie interrupted.

"We know what you mean," Margo laughingly cut off Callie.

fifteen

Theodore called last night. Said he missed me. Said he didn't understand why I was treating him the way I was. What happened between us? he asked.

C'Anne thinks I need to tell him asap. Sheila and Novel say the same thing.

But what am I supposed to do? What should I say?

Theodore thinks I'm just hiding inside my art, that I don't want to get out and deal. He thinks I'm afraid of trusting, of opening up. He thinks the art protects me.

Plus how can my art protect me from this? It can't do a damn thing about this.

It's not the art's fault, it's mine. I did think it would keep me safe. That nothing bad would happen. But now, with this, my art is where I wrestle with God. And the anger I need to sustain this ongoing fight fuels my work now. Abstracts. I can only paint abstracts now. Slashes and thick lines, dots of purple that represent my blood. There are no women's faces here in this dark place, in the shadows of these oils. I lament. I protest. I am the madness of Latosha Briggs.

Soon, I'll be saying the art helped me to not turn out like my mother. That it helped me to not go insane. My mother never had that kind of help. That's what Novel thinks, anyway.

But what difference does it make if I'm crazy or dead from HIV?

Theodore invited himself over for dinner next week. He said he still wants to see me.

I guess I'll let him come.

March 11, 1994

Last night I dreamed about Theodore. I was painting again. I was naked when he rang the buzzer. I didn't put any clothes on. I answered the door, just like that, naked. It was warm in the apartment. Warm like summer.

He wasn't surprised when I opened the door. He came and sat down on the floor where I was painting. I had yellow and green and purple streaks of paint on my thighs where I wiped my hands on my legs. My naked legs. I talked to him about the painting, what I was trying to do. The woman in the painting looked familiar, but I didn't know who she was trying to be.

Her eyes are smart, Theodore said. I looked at him. The large size of him. The strength of his hands and forearms.

God, how I liked this man. I put my bare foot on his crossed knee and pressed on it slightly. He ran his hand up my leg. He kept talking to me about the intelligence he saw in the woman's face. All the while stroking me. I kept painting. I didn't want him to stop. I opened my legs and he moved his hand over the terrain of my legs, the valley there. I was trembling by then. He kept talking. I focused on the painting while he stroked and talked, a gentle rhythm to it. He picked up one of my feet and kissed it, toes, sole, ankle. He was tickling me. I didn't laugh. I had to concentrate. Concentrate on the most beautiful man in the world. No, the painting. I had to focus on the woman's mouth. His kisses moved up my leg. I knew where this was going. And I was not afraid. He kissed my belly, below my breasts, circled my nipples. He stooped in front of me with my nipple filling his mouth. His large hands cupped my behind and squeezed. He pulled me to him. One long hug. I took the paint brush and dipped it in a pot of blue. I pulled the brush across his chest, his muscled stomach. I painted him. Drew lines on his gleaming skin. His nipples became cobalt blue, his navel, chartreuse. I painted red polka dots on his ass. He laughed when I took his penis in my hand and painted it purple, dark as the night without moon.

Rayna was distracted at work the day she was to see Theodore. She listened half-heartedly to the depressed people bemoaning their fates on the other end of the telephone line.

They act as if they have all their lives, she thought as she listened to one person after another talk about their ongoing depression.

The Worried Well. In some ways it was obscene. Their preoccupations. Their small fears. What would they do if they discovered they had to cram decades of living into a few years?

Rayna avoided Novel at lunchtime. She wanted to be alone. Wanted to figure out which words she would use that evening to tell Theodore she was infected and how he might now be infected too.

As she slowly walked the energetic streets of the Hill, she quietly mouthed the words.

"Theodore, I'm HIV positive."

"Theodore, you better get tested."

"Theodore, have you been tested for AIDS?"

Well, she thought, I have. And it's the scariest thing.

Rayna walked until she thought she had gone far enough away from the clinic to lose the scent of medication she always suspected was on her clothes. Would she smell like that if she started taking any of the AIDS medications? Would people be able to smell the sickness on her? She turned around and headed back to the clinic.

She didn't know what words she would use with Theodore that night. She just hoped she would still have the courage to tell him.

By the end of the day, Rayna decided she couldn't possibly tell him while they were inside her apartment. The silence that was sure to fill the room with its deafening roar might kill her before AIDS ever got its chance.

She pictured Theodore walking away from her, closing the door to her apartment, her life. The image of that retreating back forced her to pick up the phone. She dialed his number.

"We're still on for tonight, I hope . . . ?" he asked gently.

"Oh, yeah. We're on. I was just wondering if we could maybe meet somewhere other than my place?"

"Still scared of yourself, huh? You know I'm not coming over there to be intimate with you, if that's what you're worried about."

"No, that's not it. I'm not scared, I mean, worried about that. It's just that lately I've been feeling like the walls are pressing in on me and I'd like to get out in the open somewhere, somewhere where there's a lot of space."

"Where do you have in mind?"

"How about the Seattle Center? We could walk around and get some Indian food."

"Sounds good. As long as you don't expect me to go on any of the rides."

"Why don't you want to go on the rides?"

"Scared of heights. Anything moving too high and too fast terrifies me."

"Ooh, a man who can show his vulnerable side. I like that."

"Well, you won't like it much when you see it in action."

Rayna hung up from talking to Theodore feeling a bit better. For the zillionth time she wished she had met him five years ago instead of now.

As she walked past the receptionists' desk and headed down the curved stairway, Novel popped her head over the banister.

"Hey, want to grab some dinner?"

"I can't tonight. I'm meeting Theodore."

"I thought you weren't going to see him anymore?"

"I wasn't, but he's pretty persistent. Besides, I have something I have to tell him."

"Oh. You're going to tell him tonight?"

"If I don't chicken out."

"Do you want me to come with you?"

"No. I'm a big girl. I can do this. I know I can."

"I know you can too. And you're no chicken. Let me know how it goes. I hope he doesn't act like a jerk about it."

"I've never seen him act like a jerk. But anyway, I'll let you know how it goes."

"I love you, Rayna."

"I love you, too, Novel."

Rayna walked through the small crowd at the Seattle Center toward Kiddieland. Theodore had agreed to the change of plans only if she agreed to meet him in a non-threatening area of the amusement park.

She walked over to one of the shiny orange benches and sat down. Soon, the growing anger she felt toward HIV-negative people began to surface. She watched a young couple argue near the helicopter ride, saw an angry young woman slap the bottom of her child.

In five days' time they won't even remember what they were angry about, she thought. What a waste of energy.

"Well, this looks safe enough. Am I late?"

Rayna turned toward the sound of Theodore's voice behind her.

"No, I'm early," she said, trying to look him over without his noticing. He towered over Rayna with his dark wool coat and shiny Italian shoes. She had forgotten how lovely his large eyes were.

"It didn't take me as long to walk here as I thought it would."

"May I sit or do you want to walk around?"

"Oh, we can walk." Rayna jumped up and started walking nervously down the walkway.

"Hey, I didn't mean to scare you off," Theodore joked. "Wait for me."

The anxiety that rose inside Rayna's stomach like a pack of startled birds began to slowly subside as they walked around the park.

Theodore grabbed her hand and stroked it with his forefinger as they walked.

"I've missed you," he said. "I want you to tell me what I did to upset you."

"Oh, Theodore. Not now. Let's just enjoy the stroll."

"How long do you want me to wait? You haven't returned my telephone calls or responded to the notes I've mailed for months. I think I at least deserve a small explanation, even if it's a lie."

"I'm not going to lie to you."

"Good. Then you have to tell me the truth, Rayna. I like you a lot, but I can't keep knocking my head against the wall trying to figure you out. I thought we got along."

"You thought we had good sex, that's not the same thing as getting along. We really haven't known each other all that long."

"I've known you long enough to know how much I enjoy being with you. And that doesn't have anything to do with sex."

Rayna glared at him.

"Well, maybe a little. But what's wrong with that?"

"There's more to relationships than sex. Sex can be great, but do we trust each other? Can I tell you my secrets and will you trust me with yours? Have we known each other long enough for that kind of intimacy?"

Theodore frowned and looked at her.

"What? Do you think I'm seeing other women besides you? Is that what all of this is about?"

"No. That's not it."

"You know, Rayna, I told you I was going to graduate school when I first met you. My studies take up a lot of my time. And then there's my job. I don't have time to be fooling around with a lot of women. You're the only woman in my life now."

"Why do men always think that everything is about them? That all a woman is concerned about is what other women they're sleeping with. Did I say anything to you about exclusivity? Did I tell you I didn't expect you to date anyone besides me? Did I say you were the only man I was going out with?"

"Yeah, you did say that. So, is that what all of this is about? You're seeing someone else?"

"Why do men always think if something's wrong, a woman is going to another man? A man is the last person I'd go to if something was wrong. I can't believe how self-centered and narrow you men are."

"Now wait a minute. Wait a minute. I didn't come all the way down here to take abuse about being a man. You're generalizing and you wouldn't appreciate it one bit if I started talking about what women do, like all women do the same thing."

"I can't tell you anything. I can't talk to you."

"Oh, you can screw me, but you can't talk to me. What kind of sense does that make? Tell me what's wrong with you."

They stood in front of the Ferris wheel. Rayna grabbed Theodore by the hand.

"If you want to talk, let's go."

"Where are we going?"

"Do you trust me?"

Theodore looked up into the sky at the buckets of people swinging in the air. A tremor went through his body beneath his long coat. He shook his head as if clearing it of water. He squeezed Rayna's hand. "Let's go."

Rayna bought two tickets for the Ferris wheel. They didn't speak as they waited their turn to enter the seat. Theodore kept the same amount of pressure on Rayna's hand. It comforted her somehow, the touch of his palm, the warmth of his skin.

It was now their turn. Both of them stepped gingerly into the bucket. The young man smiled as he locked the bar that would hold them inside the seat.

"Have a good ride," he said.

Neither Rayna nor Theodore spoke as they moved into the air, hundreds of feet above the heads of the people moving like colorful swirls of light below them.

They continued to hold hands. Rayna looked at the buildings, the sun setting in the west, painting the sky with its russet-filled fingers.

Theodore looked straight ahead, barely breathing.

Once they reached the top, the wheel stopped. They rocked back and forth in the bucket, moving as gently, as easily as if they were on top of the world.

Rayna turned and looked at Theodore's frightened face.

"Theodore, I just found out I'm HIV positive. That's why I've been avoiding you. I was ashamed and afraid. I didn't know what to say, didn't want to think that I might have infected you. But I might have. You're going to have to get tested."

Theodore gave Rayna's hand a squeeze. He looked as if he would say something, but he did not.

All of Rayna's fears about telling him rushed to her lips; she opened her mouth to free them.

Theodore took his hand and put his fingers to her lips, shushing her. He pointed to the ground and nodded his head.

"What?" Rayna asked.

Once again Theodore pointed toward the ground and nodded his head.

"I don't understand what you're trying to say," Rayna said.

"The ground. I'll talk to you on the ground," Theodore mumbled and laid his head on the back of the seat.

Once the Ferris wheel stopped and they were safely back on the ground, Theodore began to pull Rayna quickly behind him toward the exit.

"Hey, slow down a minute," Rayna began. But Theodore stopped and jerked his body around until he was standing directly in front of Rayna with a look of intense anger on his face. For one brief moment, Rayna saw the end of the world inside Theodore's eyes.

"I know better than this. You know better. I used a jimmy most of the time," he said, pacing. "We could both end up dead, here. You want trust, you want secrets?" he ground out between his teeth.

For a moment Rayna was frightened. Theodore had the same look on his face that Danny had had the one time he lost control and wrapped his fingers around Rayna's throat and squeezed until she couldn't breathe and she had dropped to the ground. Never again, she had told herself then, and prepared to get away from Theodore now, as quickly as she could.

"My brother died of AIDS," he continued. "Is that a big enough secret for you?"

Rayna stopped pulling away from Theodore and stood completely still, listening to what he was saying, and what was beneath his words, unsaid.

"My brother, Powell, died alone. Shunned by his family. My mother and father were so afraid people would find out Powell was gay and had AIDS that they stayed away from him when he was dying and made him stay away from us. I was just as bad as they were, just as scared, just as trifling. Worried about what my boys would say 'cause he was gay. Maybe they'd think I was too.

"I called him a punk to his face when he told me he was gay. Called him a punk and told him to leave me the fuck alone. Didn't want nothing to do with him. Then when my mama told me he had AIDS, I didn't do nothing, didn't say nothing, didn't visit, didn't call, nothing. I'm gonna take that with me to the grave. My own brother, and I didn't even try to be there for him."

Rayna had to stop looking at the pain in Theodore's eyes. She rubbed his hand with both of hers.

"You know, Theodore, this disease makes cowards out of all of us."

"But I don't want to go out of the world like that, Rayna. That's what a punk is and I finally learned my brother wasn't no punk. That's why I decided to study public health. I've got to do what I can do to stop the spread of AIDS and maybe to help find a cure."

"Why didn't you tell me this before, Theodore?"

"I've told a few people and some of them started to act like I had AIDS, just because my brother did, like it runs in families or something. I wanted to wait to see if you would run away from me too."

"Well, now you know I've got it. How are you going to start treating me?"

Theodore pulled her over to a nearby bench. They sat silently for a moment.

"I get tested every year. Been negative so far. I'll get another one in six months or so."

"What if you get AIDS, like your brother? What would you do? I bet you can't even imagine what it feels like to have HIV. Be there for the cure, they tell you. How easy the words fall from their negative lips. Do they really know what it feels like to be a leper? Do they even care beyond the platitudes and words offering solace?"

He reached for one of Rayna's hands and squeezed it. "How are you doing with this?"

"I'm not running around town screaming and crying like a crazy woman anymore."

"Do you know who you got it from?"

"I have my suspicions, but I haven't been able to find him to ask him about any of this."

They sat quietly for a while until Rayna felt Theodore's anger begin to lessen.

"You should do something," Theodore said at last.

"Do what?" Rayna asked. "Run for a political office? Join a sorority? Quit my job working at a clinic responsible for counseling HIV positive women to get sterilized and start marching with the Prejudice Posse?"

"You can do all or none of that. I know a woman who

takes care of children with AIDS. You could go to her and do your art with those children."

Rayna stood and glared at Theodore.

"What do I know about children with AIDS?"

"Just remember what you were like when you were a kid and be like that. Open, full of wonder and free."

"But these kids are dying," Rayna said. "How can I look them in the eyes and tell them anything but the truth?"

"They already know the truth," Theodore said. "You won't be the one to have to tell them. Besides, it's always good to get out of ourselves and our own little lives. Maybe that's the beauty of this disease. It will push us so far outside of ourselves that we'll finally see how connected we are with everybody else living in the world."

Rayna looked at the earnestness inside Theodore's eyes. Where she had only moments ago imagined him crushing her with the strength of his large hands, now she could sense how much he wanted to hold her. He placed his arm gently around her shoulder and urged her up from the bench.

"I go to Mrs. Jenkins's house every week. Why don't you come with me tomorrow. You can meet her and the kids and talk to her about doing an art workshop there."

Rayna hesitated.

"You can talk to the kids about everything other than death," Theodore said as they walked slowly from the park.

March 12, 1994

I told Theodore I was positive last night. On the Ferris wheel. At the top of the world. He was more afraid of the height than what I had to tell him.

His brother died of AIDS.

Sheila calls what Theodore has "survivor's guilt." Theodore has always felt guilty. His work with Mrs. Jenkins and her Dancing Unicorn House kids helps him with that. But I can't help wondering, How do you look into the eyes of a dying child and stay sane?

Theodore wants to keep seeing me.

When we got back to my apartment, I lit my candles and we sat on the area rug on the living room floor. Theodore took off his coat, but left the rest of his clothes on. I had on my denim skirt and black tights. My sweater without a bra.

We don't have to be afraid of loving, he said. This is not the time to be without touch, he said. Now is when we need it more than ever. And I'm not talking about sex, I'm talking about touch, he said.

He took my hands in his and kissed them. I started to feel afraid for him. He placed my hands on his face and shook his head until I stopped being afraid. He laid me down on the rug. He slipped off my shoes, pulled down my tights. He brushed his lips gently across my toes, then kissed each one. He raised my leg and brushed his mustache across my ankle, over the soles of my feet. His breath was hot when he blew on my calf. It tickled. He trailed his tongue along the inside of my thigh and I started to squirm.

You want me to stop? he asked.

What could I do but moan?

He ran his hands over my behind under my skirt, squeezing, kneading, caressing. He put his head under my skirt and planted kisses around the edges of my panties.

Wait, I said. Wait.

He stopped.

His lips had branded my skin. Don't stop, I said, remembering Sheila and Janice's encouraging words. I am alive and a sensual being. I am entitled to this pleasure.

I felt so alive beneath the warmth of his breath. His lips made me think about anything but death.

Theodore helped me remove my sweater. He traced circles around my navel, then slid his tongue to my nipples where he took one, then the other, between his teeth. He kissed my stomach before he blew his breath on my neck. My legs began to shake.

Just a minute, he said.

I was still, but my body was making a sound something like humming.

Theodore returned with the Kama Sutra massage oil. Chocolate Mint. He opened it and told me to lie on my stomach. His hands smoothed the oil on my body, into my hungry skin. He held my calves, thighs, buttocks in his hands and stroked them, massaged my back until not one knot of tension remained. Easily, he rubbed my neck, pushed his tongue into my ear, rolled me over and massaged the front of my body, my thighs, my stomach, my breasts, my shoulders, and then when I was nothing but honey beneath his hands, he laid his body on top of me and we lay like that until I started to rub myself against him, against the rough texture of the pants that covered his muscled thigh, then I pushed myself against his body until he lay beneath me and I was astride him and able to ride until I reached a land where there was no AIDS, no terror, no secrets, only this grinding pleasure, this wicked wetness between my legs.

And that's just a taste of what safer sex can be like, he said.

We lay on that rug for hours breathing together, licking, rubbing, holding, being still. It was as if the HIV had broken something open in our relationship; there was no room for lying or secrets. There was not even space for promises. Those, I told him, are forbidden. He made me promise to meet Mrs. Jenkins and her kids, though. So I will do it. For myself and for Theodore.

How could I say no to a man who can caress me with words like that?

sixteen

Rayna sat doodling at her desk, watching people walk down the brick pathway into the clinic. Novel popped her head into the office.

"So how did it go with Theodore?"

Rayna smiled.

"Don't give me that hussyette smile. What happened? He must not have freaked or you wouldn't be looking so happy."

"No. He didn't react at all like I thought he would. I'm telling you, I wish I had met him ten years ago. I wouldn't have wasted my time with so many of those other fools."

"Live and learn. Live and learn."

"But I don't have a lot more time for learning."

"You know what I mean." Novel walked over to Rayna and gently grabbed her hand. "Besides, even death can be a learning experience."

"I wish you would take this course and tell me all about it, then."

Rayna jumped up from her desk when she saw the wounded look on Novel's face. She gave her friend a tight hug.

"I didn't mean to hurt you, Rayna. I just meant to say that I've heard a lot of dying people say that the experience changed their lives in a radical way for the better."

"I know, I've heard that too. But it's still hard to listen to somebody say it. I wouldn't want anyone I know to trade places with me. You know that. I wouldn't mind Dr. Van Horne stepping in these shoes right about now, but he's the only one I can think of to wish this on."

"Did you hear the latest about the Briggs case?"

"No, girl. You know how hush-hush that's become around here. Joy turns red as a beet any time I try to bring it up."

"Well, you know they're going to treat us as if we might turn traitor on them any minute. It turns out two more women have come forward to say that Dr. Van Horne pressured them into getting sterilized and they never signed consent forms. Both of them are HIV positive. And of course the hospital is backing Van Horne all the way. It makes me so mad. And those women don't have money to fight this thing."

"There must be some kind of way to get corroborative evidence against him without getting ourselves into trouble," Rayna said.

"But what could we do? I know one of his nurses, but she wouldn't do anything to hurt that man, even if he was sterilizing her sisters. She thinks he's God."

"But would she let you in the vicinity of his files?" Rayna asked. "So I could copy the consent forms and turn them over to the Prejudice Posse?"

"You know they would put us under the jail if they ever found out about it, though. Right?" Novel asked.

"If they ever found out that is probably what they would do. You can't afford to take the risk."

"Rayna, neither can you. You know how this machine works. It'll grind you into nothing. Your life will be ruined."

The two women looked at each other. They hugged again as Rayna smiled and shook her head.

Rayna decided she would wait to tell Theodore about the plan she and Novel had come up with to expose Dr. Van Horne. She trusted Theodore more than she had ever trusted any man, but she still didn't want him to try to talk her out of it.

This would be the first time she had ever become involved in anything close to criminal. Smoking dope didn't count. The thought of handling those confidential doctors' files made the hair on her arms stand on end.

She noticed she was now walking with a stealthier gait, slow, easy, loose-limbed. She rolled lightly on the balls of her feet. Even in her Birkenstocks.

She didn't want her face to give away her slit-eyed secrets. She felt like a bumbling detective in a B movie.

Finally, she made herself stop thinking about what she had to do. The Watergate burglars never regarded what they had done as a crime. Why should she?

Innocent women were having their privacy invaded, their rights taken away. All because of the virus in their blood. The same virus that ran wild through her blood.

Who would have the courage to stop them from doing it to her?

After work, she ran down the curved stairway and out the front door of the clinic. She had to walk five blocks to Mrs. Jenkins's house, where she was to meet Theodore. Five blocks was plenty of time to cement the Van Horne plan firmly inside her mind. After they found out the names of the additional women accusing Dr. Van Horne, Rayna would accompany Novel into the central file room at Central Hospital under the guise of looking for a patient-in-crisis medical file. Due to the emergency nature of the situation they would be able to circumvent the normal procedure for requesting files. Once they were able to get their hands on the women's files, Rayna would copy them and reshelve them.

As long as the files were actually filed away and not buried in Van Horne's office, she shouldn't have any problems making the copies. It wouldn't be too difficult to locate the Prejudice Posse and mail them the information. She would send it anonymously, though it would be difficult to remain silent once the administration determined Van Horne had to have been exposed by coworkers.

She would have to act soon, while she was not frightened.

"Took you long enough," Theodore called out from the front porch of the mammoth lime-green Victorian with a sign over the door that read: DANCING UNICORN HOUSE. From the simple lines and colors Rayna guessed some of the children must have painted the sign.

"Don't you start with me, now," Rayna responded with a short laugh.

"You better be on your best behavior. Mrs. Jenkins doesn't take no mess."

Theodore grabbed Rayna's hand and pulled her up the steps. He knocked lightly on the door.

"It's Theo, Mrs. Jenkins," he called as he walked inside. Rayna followed, shyly.

"We're in here," a woman's voice called from deep inside the house.

"Dinnertime. This way you'll get a chance to see how much the kids do normal kid stuff. Makes you less afraid of them."

"Who said I was afraid?"

"Well, maybe it's me who's got your hand sweating."

Rayna snatched her hand away from Theodore's grasp and shoved it in the pocket of her pants.

They moved from the darkness of the wood-paneled walls into the brightly painted kitchen. Mrs. Jenkins certainly loved lime green. The cabinets were painted lime, the linoleum had flecks of lime, even the long wooden table had lime-colored tiles in its center.

"I'm blasting them with light, honey," Mrs. Jenkins said as she watched Rayna examine her kitchen. "Blasting them with light and love. You must be Rayna. Theodore's been telling us a lot about you. Have a seat."

"Theo. Theo. We going to the park, Theo?"

Theodore was obviously well loved in this house. Rayna watched as he gave each child a hug or high five.

Rayna looked at the five children seated at the table. All but one looked like any other kid she would normally ignore on the street. Clean, well-fed, happy.

"We take all kinds of children here," Mrs. Jenkins continued. "Black, red, brown, yellow. AIDS doesn't discriminate. But I guess you know that by now."

Rayna didn't respond as she took a seat next to the skinniest child she had ever seen. The girl turned her large dark eyes on Rayna.

"Mrs. Jenkins says in Africa what I got is called slim. You

got slim?" the girl asked Rayna. Rayna nodded her head.

"My name is Anika. What's yours?"

"Rayna." The thinness of the girl's arms, the large liquid surface of her dark eyes, the serenity in her small, reedy voice unnerved Rayna.

"Rayna is thinking about coming and showing you some fancy art tricks. Do you think you'd like that?" Mrs. Jenkins asked the children.

"YEAH! YAY! OK!" the children yelled, all at once, in one voice, five different yesses.

Mrs. Jenkins then turned to Rayna.

"Do you think you'd like that? We don't promise the children anything that we can't follow through on. I understand you haven't worked much with children. And these are very special children. I fight with everything I've got not to let anything or anyone unnecessarily hurt them. They've got enough on their plates as it is. Make sure you are strong enough, woman enough to say yes to them before you even try to mouth the word."

Mrs. Jenkins then turned to Theodore.

"So how have you been, Theo? Have you told Rayna all about us, all about Dancing Unicorn House? Does she know about me?"

"I left that story for you to tell, Mrs. Jenkins."

She turned back to Rayna. "My husband died of AIDS ten years ago. Back then, there wasn't the support or help there is today. I didn't know what was wrong with him. The doctors barely knew. Toward the end, he kept getting sicker and going in and out of the hospital. Had something growing like moss all over his body. Finally, they told me what it was. I was scared to death. For him. For myself. I couldn't tell anybody what he had. How he got it didn't matter to me. I was his wife. Had been for twenty-five years. Yes, I know he once used drugs. Yes, I know he'd laid down with just about anybody that could be laid down with. But he was my husband and I was going to stand by him no matter if it killed me. And it almost did. It almost has. I started this house for these kids with the insurance money I got when he died. What else was I going to do with it?"

"Do all of the children live here or do some of them just come here for your programs?"

"They all live here with me."

Rayna didn't know how to respond. She couldn't imagine how this woman had been able to turn so much loss into such largesse. She shook her head. Mrs. Jenkins reached for Rayna's hand across the table. She grabbed it and gave it a firm squeeze.

"You are going to be all right, Rayna. You are going to be just fine."

Mrs. Jenkins's touch was an anointing. Her fingertips stroked Rayna's temples, easing the tension away. The healing balm of her words cascaded over Rayna's bowed head, soothing her, washing her tainted blood clean.

When she released Rayna's hand, Rayna felt as if she had been on the mourner's bench, as if she had fallen on her knees and emptied her heart of all its troubles into the cup of blessings of Mrs. Jenkins's lap.

"Yes," Rayna told Mrs. Jenkins and Theodore and Anika and all of the other children she would come to know and love over the following months. Yes, she was woman enough to come and work with the children of Dancing Unicorn House.

seventeen

"This doesn't sound like you, Rayna. I mean, you've always been so into your . . . art," C'Anne commented as they sat at Rayna's kitchen table later that evening.

"You mean myself. I've always been too into myself to care about spending a lot of time with somebody else. I know you, C'Anne. You can say it. I won't be offended. It's the truth."

"It's not that. Your art needs a lot of time. I don't think there is such a thing as an unselfish artist. And I don't mean that as a criticism," C'Anne said, fingering the pepper shaker shaped like a slice of watermelon. "I'm just surprised how easily you've let Theodore into your space."

"Theodore isn't living with me or anything . . ."

"Yet."

"It's too soon for anything like that to happen. I don't have time now to try to figure out what I would do with a man in my space. But it's nice having him around sometimes. You know how good it can feel to wake up next to someone."

"Yeah, but you've got the bonus of waking up to someone

who has his own place to go to when he's getting on your nerves. I don't have that."

Rayna chuckled.

"I think I'm not going to be able to put so much time into my painting anymore, C'Anne. There's so much going on now and I feel so tired most of the time."

"Are you going to try to get involved in any research trials so you can get some free treatment?" C'Anne asked.

"I looked into it, but most of them are focused on men. If you have a uterus, they don't want you. They're too afraid of what a drug might do to an unborn child, even if you swear you don't have any plans to have children."

"But what about working with those kids? Are you going to have enough energy for that? What about your own health? Are you up to all of this?"

"I'm going to do that. I want to do that. I'm going to find a way to show them how art can help them to understand life. You should have seen those sweet little faces, C'Anne. And all of them are going to die."

Rayna stood and walked to the whistling tea kettle on the stove to hide her tears.

"We're all going to die one day, Rayna," C'Anne said, frowning. "Spending time painting with those kids when you're sick yourself isn't going to stop any of their deaths. And the stress may cause you to get sick sooner."

"But I need to do something," Rayna said as she poured the steaming tea into two mismatched coffee mugs. "Something for all of us. Something that will make a difference before I go. I just can't see myself dying in a few years and all I'll have left behind is a roomful of painted canvases."

Rayna placed the hot mugs gingerly on the table and sat down.

"Maybe you and Theodore will have a baby," C'Anne said wistfully. "Even with a fifty-fifty chance, you could try."

Rayna stood up. She began pacing the small square of white linoleum, then stopped abruptly, dropped her head, and sighed.

"I'm never going to have a baby, C'Anne. You know that. We all know that. Even if I'd ever wanted to have one, which I didn't, I can't have one now. Not with this disease."

"You have a fifty-fifty chance of giving birth to a HIV negative baby."

"I couldn't do that to the child or to myself. If the child is negative then I risk leaving it motherless, and if it's positive I could never forgive myself. And I know Theodore wouldn't go along with it. He could get infected by having unprotected sex with me. And then we'd all have the peculiar pleasure of watching each other die. I couldn't even stand the thought."

"You've got a lot of years left, Rayna. You can't think and act as if it's already over," C'Anne said as she stood and walked toward Rayna. "And cutting back on your art now, after all these years and heartache, just doesn't make any sense to me. You can use your art for healing if you want, healing yourself and others. Cutting yourself off from one of the things that has sustained you most in life seems ridiculous, and, frankly, overdramatic." C'Anne reached for Rayna's hand and stroked it. "I hope you give it more thought."

"Thanks for holding yourself back and sparing my feelings," Rayna said, laughing.

"It's good to hear you laugh again. But you know I've always envied your life as an artist. I've been living vicariously through you all of these years. When I hit bottom with my drinking, I didn't have anything the way you have your art to pull yourself through. If you stop being my art connection, where will I get it in my life?"

"Maybe you'll just develop your own connection, C'Anne."

They both sat at the table once again. Rayna began to tilt her chair on its hind legs. C'Anne drank her tea silently for a moment.

"What does Novel think about all of this? She's certainly been making herself scarce."

Rayna dropped the chair's legs to the ground.

"I don't know what Novel thinks. It's interesting. She's gotten really therapeutic on me. She hooked me up with the support group, gave me pamphlets to read, people I could call for information. She was the first one I told and she put all of her therapist skills to work on me and it's been great. We went to central files at Central Hospital and located the information I needed for the Prejudice Posse. Latosha Briggs's file wasn't there. Dr. Van Horne probably has it under lock and key, but we found the other two women's files. I made copies and mailed them to the Prejudice Posse. Novel was game. She was right there with me but I didn't let her touch those files. We need her to stay working at the clinic. And I know it's hard for her to deal with this. I've had to handle my own fears right now and she knows that."

Rayna stared into the honey-colored liquid in her mug.

"You know death and illness always strike people in different ways," C'Anne said. "The same way going to a hospital does. I know people who won't go into a hospital no matter who is sick inside. Something about it makes death real for them, too real. They can't go in and pretend like they're avoiding dying or debilitation or getting old.

"Novel loves you and I know she doesn't know what to do, despite her therapeutic skills. None of us was prepared for AIDS to strike this close to home. Maybe I'll have a hen party sometime soon, and we can talk about all of this. Get everything out in the open."

"That would be nice, C'Anne. I love it that you still think of me as I used to be, unchanged."

"Everything has changed, Rayna. I know that. But let me have the right to a little of my own denial. And some fun. You know how I love to get together with you fast hussy-ettes."

"C'Anne, you know you're faster than any of us by a good mile." Rayna smiled into the eyes of her friend.

C'Anne laughed.

"I guess I better ease on out of here," C'Anne said, as she rose from the table and walked toward the front door. "I promised Mr. P. I'd bake him a peach cobbler today."

Rayna cooed as she followed C'Anne to the door.

"Mmm. Um. It's been so long since I've had an appetite for any food. I eat now just to keep my body going."

"Well, I'll save you a big piece," C'Anne said. "I don't know what cobbler will do for your immune system, but I know it will be chock-full of love."

At the door, the two women clung to each other, and as C'Anne turned to walk away, Rayna saw a trace of tears glistening on C'Anne's dark cheeks.

*   *   *

April 4, 1994

Circe called today. She wants to know when they can meet Theodore. Says Car wants to know what kind of man wants to be with a woman like me.

I told her Theodore is not like any of the other men they've met. Told her he likes to tell me about myself all the time. He gets me to thinking. Gets me to thinking about change.

Circe said I've made it this far and have been doing all right. What do I need a man to tell me about myself for? She wouldn't let no man tell her nothing. And that goes double for Car.

It isn't like that, I try to tell her. I need people in my life who are going to tell me the truth. I don't have any time left for lies.

I've been stripped down to my bones. What I look like, what I wear, what radio station I listen to, none of that matters. I could be called leper, whore, junkie, bloodsucker, dyke, Rayna, unholy one. None of those names matters. I have been stripped. I have been cleansed. In the icy grip of death, I have been reborn.

Circe and Car want us to come to dinner. Maybe I'll ask Theodore. Maybe we'll . . .

The first Saturday afternoon Rayna was to lead her art workshop at Dancing Unicorn House, she woke up with a tickle in her throat.

Damn, she thought. She would have to call Mrs. Jenkins to cancel the workshop. She couldn't take a chance on making one of the children sick.

"Sore throat, huh?" Mrs. Jenkins asked.

"Yeah, I woke up with it. I don't want to make one of the kids sick."

"Uh-huh" was all Mrs. Jenkins said.

"I'm really disappointed. I've been looking forward to this all week."

"You don't say," Mrs. Jenkins said.

Rayna had the distinct feeling that Mrs. Jenkins hadn't listened to a word she had said.

Finally, Mrs. Jenkins spoke.

"You know the kids have been waiting on you all week long. We got plenty of masks you could put on while you show them what to do. That is, if you really want to come."

Rayna was surprised at the burst of anger that swelled inside the pit of her belly at Mrs. Jenkins's words. Of course she really wanted to come. She didn't want to let the kids down. Theodore would never let her forget it.

"I'll be there at two, like I said I would," Rayna said as she slammed the phone into the receiver.

Rayna trekked to Dancing Unicorn House carrying a large canvas bag filled with various art supplies. She had decided to use fabric scraps and a glue gun to make some pieces they could call their ancestors.

Mrs. Jenkins had agreed to save white plastic gallon bottles that they could cover and turn into faces.

Mrs. Jenkins met Rayna at the front door and placed a mask carefully over Rayna's nose and mouth. She hurried

Rayna into the kitchen. Five expectant faces turned to look at Rayna.

"Children, here is Theo's friend Rayna. You remember, she's an artist and has come here to teach you something about art. I hope you'll pay good attention and mind. You can introduce yourselves when I leave.

"Rayna woke up with a tickle in her throat this morning, so she is going to wear a mask today so she won't spread any germs. Does anybody have any questions before I leave the room?"

The children looked at Rayna.

"Listen carefully to what Rayna has to say, children. It's going to be a little bit hard to hear what she is saying clearly. But I want you to try hard. She is going to."

Mrs. Jenkins quietly left the kitchen.

"Do you have slim?" the small-boned girl, Anika, asked Rayna again.

Rayna nodded. She felt as if the mask were suffocating her. She breathed deeply inside it.

Rayna was terrified as she removed her supplies from the bag and placed them at the center of the table. Still, she loved the texture of the woods, the softness of the brushes, the radiant colors of the scraps. As she touched the tools she had used to create new worlds, her fear began to subside. She could give the children a sense of peace and beauty and power.

At first she didn't know if she was more afraid of collapsing from not being able to breathe inside the mask or from trying to teach these dying children about life.

She groaned quietly as she realized that she had now become the masked woman in her paintings.

Anika came and sat next to Rayna. She turned those all-seeing eyes on Rayna's trembling hands.

"I shake too," she said. "See?"

Anika's hands hung limply at the ends of her thin wrists. How could a child get this thin in America? Rayna wondered. She could imagine this thinness in countries where famine and desolation from warring tribes existed, but not here in this sunny, warm, lime-green kitchen in Mrs. Jenkins's house.

Rayna spoke as clearly as she could through the gauzy fabric of the mask.

"A lot of people think art has to be painting pictures, but it's not. Art can be a lot of things."

"Like crayons?" Francisco asked.

"Yes, crayons make art. Today I'm going to show you how to make some art out of those old plastic bottles Mrs. Jenkins uses for milk."

"Milk art?" Davida asked.

"In a way," Rayna responded. "We're going to take something that we usually use one way and use it in another way. Does anybody know what that's called?"

"Art," Anika said proudly.

"Yes, that's right. It's called recycled art. And it's called recycled art because we find a way to use it over and over again.

"What I want us to do now is pick out some pieces of fabric that you like and then think of someone who is very special to you who isn't alive anymore. Then I want you to take one of these markers and draw that person's face on your plastic bottle. That's going to be your ancestor. Who knows what an ancestor is?"

"Like a gramma or grampa," Gerald said.

"Yes, you're right. It's someone who has lived and died before we lived and died. In some places in the world, people believe that we are not brand-new when we're born, but that we are our ancestors, reborn. That the thoughts and lives of our ancestors are woven inside us and in that way our ancestors live on inside us. That way there is no death and no one ever really dies."

"Like my mama isn't really dead?" Anika asked.

"Not as long as you remember her, she's not. She'll always live on inside you."

"And when we die someone will remember us?" Enuya asked.

"Yes, and then you'll always live on inside them. And it goes on and on like that forever."

Rayna was amazed at how easy it had been to share these words with the children. Mrs. Jenkins had told her to feel free to talk with the children about anything. They hadn't started crying or screaming as she had envisioned, but were now busily and happily creating their ancestors. Except for Anika. She kept her slight body perched beside Rayna the entire hour, holding Rayna's hand, never once letting it go.

eighteen

I have been spending a lot of time at Dancing Unicorn House. I stop by some evenings after work, every Saturday and Sunday.

Sometimes I do a craft project with the kids, most times I just help out around the place, trying to make myself useful.

Theodore thinks I'm coming around. That there's a human being somewhere inside me, under the lingering paint fumes and the permanent coloring beneath my fingernails.

I'm feeling good. Most of the children are relatively healthy. Except Anika. She is in the late stages of the disease, Mrs. Jenkins says. I don't believe it, though. She is bright and full of questions. She clings to me like a second skin while I'm there.

Next Tuesday will be her tenth birthday. She made me

promise to take her to the park and teach her how to play baseball.

That's the one thing she wishes for, she says. To be able to play ball like the other kids.

Mrs. Jenkins says Anika is so small, she is too weak to throw or catch the ball. Anika looks at me with those moon eyes. I tell her I will try.

"Will you be my mommy?"

Rayna looked sharply toward the pitcher's mound into Anika's searching eyes. She could not imagine what Anika saw when she looked at Rayna. What would make her think Rayna could mother her? Bright angels above, this child probably wouldn't live to see her eleventh birthday.

"But Mrs. Jenkins is your mommy, Anika," Rayna replied, dodging the question. The sun seemed to be shining brighter into Rayna's eyes. The dust from Anika's kicking feet drifted lazily across the field.

"Here, catch this one," Rayna yelled as she threw the softball gently toward Anika's outstretched hand. The left-handed baseball glove, big as Anika's head, weighed her arm down.

She dropped the ball.

"See, I told you, I'm never gonna learn how to catch the ball. They're never gonna pick me to play on the team," Anika said disgustedly, as she threw the ball at Rayna.

Mrs. Jenkins had told Rayna the children at school didn't

know Anika had AIDS. The principal and Anika's teacher, Mrs. Gordon, didn't think it was necessary for the entire school to know.

"It's probably for the best," Mrs. Jenkins had said to them, nodding her head as if listening to the encouraging words of a preacher.

"It's not the kids I'm worried about, it's their parents," Mrs. Gordon had said. "They'd probably turn their kids against Anika before they even knew anything about her. I don't want to give her up to that kind of ignorance and fear. She's got enough on her plate."

"Didn't you see how those white folks did that family down in Florida? Burned their house down to the ground so those boys wouldn't go to school with their children. What kind of way is that for children to live out their last days?" Mrs. Jenkins had asked them.

"Try catching it with both hands," Rayna said. "Grab the ball with your mitt, then put your other hand over the ball."

Rayna picked the rolling ball up from the ground and tossed it again to Anika.

Though she had always felt pity when she saw news stories about children with AIDS, she had never imagined it touching her world. Had never even dreamed that anyone she might care about would ever be ravaged by this disease.

AIDS was a news story, a thirty-second sound bite, a hideous photograph in a glossy magazine, not this frowning, honey-colored child desperately trying to learn how to catch a ball so she could fit in at her school. Not this girl-child wanting Rayna, of all people, to be her mother.

Rayna, a woman who had said she would never be anyone's wife again or anyone's mother, a woman who loved a world of thickly textured paint and canvas, silky-haired brushes, the pattern of light falling through the window, the unparalleled exhilaration of creating nebulous things of beauty, this woman voluntarily imprisoned inside her tortured imaginings, had decided long ago she would never have enough of herself to give to anyone or anything other than her art.

Plus, she was afraid of mothers.

Rayna's real mother hadn't been able to take care of herself. She forgot what day it was, the time of day, whether or not she or Rayna had eaten. She didn't wash herself or Rayna. Hadn't believed in cleaning. That's what they had all told Rayna anyway. Her mother heard things other people couldn't: birds quarreling, dogs praying, angels singing inside her ears.

Rayna did not want the same thing to happen to her.

When Rayna was nineteen and lying on a metal table with her legs gapped and her heels in steel stirrups, she remembered the way the sun had beaten down on the playground when she looked up into the sky as the kids had circled her and that bully, Crayfish, waiting for the first blow to fall.

But there had been no fight in her then, as there was none in her as she lay helpless on that table with the doctor working quickly at the foot of it.

Ice. The room had made her think of ice, frost everywhere, even on the doctor's fingertips as he inserted his hand inside her and calculated dimensions. His cool blue eyes had never looked directly into hers.

One minute she had heard the clicking of the speculum and the next the sucking of the machine as it pulled what could one day have been a life from her trembling body.

"Now you're not pregnant anymore," the doctor had said as he wiped his hands on the tan paper towel the nurse mechanically offered him. They both then had turned and left the room.

How could she create with a man or a child around? Underfoot. Wanting your attention. Needing you.

Rayna had had several abortions since she was nineteen and only now began to regret at least one of those decisions. It had not entered her consciousness that she would never be able to have children if she changed her mind.

Though she had sympathized and cluck-cluck-clucked with C'Anne and her other friends who were fast approaching or passing forty and still childless and feeling their time had just about run out, she had never understood the pressure they felt.

Weren't their lives enough? What did they believe a child was going to add to their lives?

Now, for the first time, Rayna understood.

Anika was a terminally ill child. A sick child. Even though it had been several months since her last stay in the hospital, everyone knew she'd soon return. Anika was no longer HIV positive, she had moved into full-blown AIDS.

Rayna didn't know how to cope with her own impending deterioration. How could she possibly help Anika?

Lost in her own thoughts, Rayna didn't see the ball coming straight toward her head. Too late, she raised her hand and turned her head, but the ball caught her on the right temple. She fell on her knees to the ground.

"Hey, you should've said something, Anika. Didn't you see I wasn't ready for the ball?"

Anika didn't answer. Rayna raised her head and looked at the small child standing ten feet away. Rayna couldn't read the expression on Anika's face.

"Well, aren't you going to say you're sorry?" Rayna asked.

Anika threw her mitt down and started to walk off the field.

"Anika. Where are you going?"

Anika continued her stiff-legged walk away from Rayna.

"Are you all right?"

Rayna slowly stood and massaged her temple as she started to follow Anika.

"Do you hear me talking to you?"

Anika started to trot.

Rayna picked up her pace. She didn't want to have to chase Anika down.

"Anika!"

Anika broke into a gallop. She ran off the baseball diamond, across the asphalt, toward the steps leading to a steep embankment of trees.

Rayna started running behind her. She had never been a fast runner and this time was no exception. Anika easily pulled away from her and loped up the steps two at a time.

She sure doesn't run like she's dying, Rayna thought. But I'm going to die if she doesn't stop soon.

Anika turned at the top of the steps and looked back at Rayna huffing behind her. Rayna thought she saw a shadow of pity slide across Anika's face, but if it was there, it was quickly gone. In its wake was a trace of tears.

Anika sat on the top step. Rayna slowly reached the top and sat beside her. Anika folded her slight body into herself, head on crossed arms laying across her knees. First her shoulders started shaking, then Rayna heard sniffles.

Here was a nine-year-old child whose mother had been using crack since it first hit the streets of Seattle, a child who had been trying to take care of herself and got herself to school in the mornings without alarm clock or warm hands, just the knowledge that a new day had come and there would be breakfast at school if she got there early enough, often so early she beat the teachers there, a child whose mother had allowed every kind of drug and man entrance to her body and soul, then left this disease as a legacy, a disease that caused this child to be susceptible to dying from a common cold, this child who had stood at her mother's hospital bed as she lay dying and did not cry, did not rage, did not break down, but told that dying woman how much she had loved her cold-water corn bread and the way her mama could dance, this child who did not cry when she found out the disease that was going to kill her mother was going to kill her too, and she still had not cried. Now this child with a type of courage Rayna had never witnessed, this child was sitting beside her crying as if she were going to shed tears for all of the years and all of the pain and all of the things she had been too afraid to cry about before.

Rayna let her cry. She had decided long ago she would not be one of the people in Anika's life who would lie to her. She would not lie to her like the women at Mrs. Jenkins's church who had told Anika that her mother was going to get better, that she was not going to die. She would help her face the truth of her situation, unflinchingly.

She did not want Anika to end up as she had as a child, at the center of a ring of kids shouting the truth of her life to her as they stood in a circle with the sun beating down on her and its glare in her eyes. And what did any of it matter, anyway? Anika was loved. And so was Rayna.

No matter what her mother did or had done, no matter if she had never given her an ounce of food or a drop of water, Amilcar and Circe had been there for Rayna, had stepped in and given her all the love she could ever possibly need. Car alone had loved her enough for five mothers. And Mrs. Jenkins had done the same for Anika.

"But Mrs. Jenkins is everybody's mama," Anika had told Rayna one day. "I want one of my own."

Rayna pulled Anika's trembling body close to her own. She gently massaged Anika's back while Anika emptied herself.

All right, she thought wearily. I'll do it. Whatever it takes to mother this child, I'll do.

nineteen

May 24, 1994

Novel called last night. She didn't talk in her professional voice. For the first time in months, she sounded real. She cried on the phone. I heard her crying. I don't have any tears right now.

She started working on a new collage. She wants me to help her with it. I told her I didn't have much time for art anymore.

Novel said the art will save me if I let it, like music, she said. Don't turn against what you love in your heart, she said. The art didn't let you down.

My life is filled with work and children. And Theodore. He spends every minute he's not at school or working or at Dancing Unicorn House here, with me.

Yes, it's strange having someone almost living with me, I told Novel. I have to share. For the first time since my divorce, I have to share. It's an adjustment, but not impossible.

Now, Theodore sleeps with me most nights and wraps me inside his arms when my list of fears becomes not words but graven images carved into the backs of my eyelids as I dream of death.

Sometimes when I wake up, he is watching me. He imagines my nightsweats are the fevers of his brother and he holds me. Tight enough to grasp the spirit of his brother lying beside us in bed.

Theodore touches me. I told Novel. Told her we are still able to be intimate. How I've grown to love surgical gloves and have found a certain kind of sexiness in latex. A little lube inside a rubber can go a long way. Told her Glyde dental dams do feel like silk stockings.

All it takes is an imagination. And Theodore has plenty of that.

Novel says good-bye with a sadness that is so rare for her, I almost cry. But my plan to adopt Anika revives me.

Theodore doesn't agree with my plans, though. He doesn't think I'm ready to handle the emotional responsibility yet. But I'm going to do it. Mrs. Jenkins didn't say anything when I told her. I know she didn't think I could stick it out with the kids. That I'd get bored or tired of their neediness.

Both of them are wrong. I'll show them. I feel a tremendous sense of peace about my decision. Plus, Anika looks so happy.

June 10, 1994

The best thing about adopting Anika is: I will give her a home She can live out her final days knowing she is loved She is funny She is cute She always wants to hold my hand I can teach her things I can love her I can take care of her when she is sick She will know she is not alone I will know I am not alone I will give her a home I will love her like my own child I will never have children I will never live to be old and see them grow up She will never grow up She will be a child always My child She will never be an adolescent She will never have zits She will never change on me and turn into a mutant teenage terminator girl She will teach me all the latest dance steps I will teach her to appreciate jazz We will go to museums We will go to baseball games We will roller-skate and play ice hockey We will paint We will hold hands We will live forever inside our love We will live forever loved We will live forever

June 11, 1994

The worst thing about adopting Anika is: She is stubborn She is too skinny She will one day have tubes running in and out of her body She will one day grow fur and spots She will one day stop breathing I will stop breathing She will make me mad She will make me do things like clean up the place when I don't want to clean it She will make me do

things like cook dinner when I don't want to cook She will
try my patience I will try her patience and make her mad
We will both be mad and have AIDS We will both be mad
at AIDS Some days I will yell I always do Some days she
will yell Some days we both will yell and it won't be pretty
One day I will get sick too and skinny One day my skin will
be covered with fur and spots One day I will get sick too I
will make her take her medicine even when she doesn't
want to I will have to make her take her medicine even if it
hurts

July 1, 1994   9:00 A.M.

Mrs. Jenkins called to say Anika had to go to the hospital
last night. No, I can't visit 'cause I'm not next of kin. Only
next of kin will be allowed. Mrs. Jenkins won't tell me who
that is. I'm going to the hospital and make them let me in.
They will see that I am going to adopt Anika. They will see
that I love her. They will see the desperation in my eyes
and how important it is that she not be alone at a time like
this. When she is so small and ten years old and dying from
a disease I can't beat back with all of the love in the world.
They will look at me and see. They will look at me and
know. Just take one look. They will know.

July 1, 1994   9:20 A.M.

Sometimes I think the only thing keeping me sane is the
blank pages of this journal that I can fill with my own
thoughts. Uninterrupted. No one has any power in these
pages but me.

Mrs. Jenkins called again before I had my clothes on good to go to the hospital. Theodore answered the phone. "She's gone," she said. That was it. She hung up.

Theodore ran and grabbed me. I was standing with my leg raised and bent to push it into a pair of jeans. He grabbed me frozen like that and pulled me to him like he could squeeze all the life that had flown out of me in that one moment back inside my body.

I wasn't having any of that. There was no consolation in this. No consolation at all.

I screamed at him.

"You're just with me because you've got a weird desire to die so you can make it up to yourself for letting your brother die alone. You don't love me or those kids. You just love your own guilt."

"I'm not going to let you stand here and talk crazy to me," he said. "You can't blame her dying on me. I told you when you went, Mrs. Jenkins told you. If you want to be a part of those kids' world, you've gotta know that death is a part of that world. Grief is a part of that world."

"No. You knew this would happen."

"What?"

"All of it. You. Me. Anika. The love. You knew."

"This is part of what living is, Rayna. Nothing can protect you from it," he said. "I can't protect you from it."

"Then what good are you? What are you doing here?"

It wasn't until Theodore began to cry, that I could. We sat on the edge of the bed and cried.

For Anika, for his dead brother, for Mrs. Jenkins and the Dancing Unicorn House kids, for our eternal latex-filled nights, for the life together we would never live.

July 5, 1994

I got some of her ashes. Mrs. Jenkins saw to that. The memorial service was brief. I can't remember who was there. Everything passed in a blur. Theodore took the small box of some of Anika's precious things Mrs. Jenkins offered to us like a wedding present.

We went to Madison Park and stood near the Japanese Maple. Theodore opened the box and poured some of the ashes into my hands.

"She loved this place. We'll say good-bye to her spirit here."

I went to the pig Anika had loved to sit astride and scattered her ashes over Mrs. Magoo's pale granite back.

"Good-bye, Anika. I'm glad I got to be your mommy for a little while. I pray you are safe and well and nothing will hurt you ever again."

After a while, we left.

July 19, 1994

Today was my first day back at work since Anika died. I told Novel to slip the Van Horne files into my desk during lunch. I would send the Prejudice Posse the information they needed to help them with their case. Someone had to do something. Those consent forms all had the same signature on them. Van Horne was still walking around the place like he owned it and God.

What do I have to lose that hasn't already been lost?

twenty

Anika would have liked Coulon Park, Rayna knew. So much green and the rose-tinged stone. It would have reminded her of Mrs. Magoo, the sleek-skinned pig she loved to caress in Madison Park.

They had gone to Madison Park the day before Anika returned to the hospital for the last time.

"Mama Rayna, I know where I'm gonna go when I die," Anika had said calmly as she sat on the wooden bench holding Rayna's hand.

Rayna had instinctively tightened her body as if she could shield both of them from the reality of death. Rayna had tried to be honest with Anika about the true nature of the seriousness of their illness. Still, she found it difficult to admit this smiling-faced wide-eyed child was going to die.

If she had no space in her consciousness for the actuality of Anika's death, how was she going to face the eventuality of her own?

C'Anne and Novel came to Rayna's apartment a couple of days after the memorial service.

Rayna answered the door in her short silk robe. Her hair was matted to her skull and her skin had a sallow tinge.

"Girl, if I didn't know you were grieving, I'd swear you were on crack," Novel said as she gently patted Rayna's back.

"We know just the place to take an ailing spirit like yours," C'Anne said as she walked briskly toward Rayna's closet. "You don't have to wear anything fancy, all we need is a jogging suit."

Rayna pointed listlessly toward her dresser.

"Take that chanting music off the CD player now!" C'Anne commanded. Novel moved toward the machine quickly and began searching for other music to play.

"Put on some music that will bring her back into her body. Some Smokey Robinson or the Temptations, Funkadelic, anybody."

Novel located a Parliament CD and put it on.

"Pump it up," C'Anne yelled from the bathroom where she had taken Rayna to dress her.

Novel danced around the living room to the booming bass of George Clinton. Several moments later, C'Anne emerged with Rayna wearing a purple jogging suit and sneakers.

"I think we're ready. Novel, you hold her steady on the other side till we get to the car."

"Just let me turn the music off," Novel said.

The three women left the apartment, with Rayna sandwiched between as if she were a fragile package. They bustled her into the back seat of C'Anne's Camry and let her lie down.

"We don't have too far to go, Rayna. Just take it easy,"

C'Anne said as she climbed into the driver's seat. Novel slid into the passenger seat.

None of the women spoke as they drove through the light Saturday morning traffic toward downtown.

Novel laid her head on the back of the seat and covered her eyes with her arm. C'Anne shook her braids in anger at drivers who inadvertently crossed her path.

They drove toward Pike Place Market and stopped in front of the Athletic Club.

"It's about time I put our membership to good use," C'Anne said. "Mr. P. hates to exercise and so do I. But this is a special situation that calls for drastic measures. Novel, help me get Rayna out of the car."

The women pulled and tugged at Rayna until she stood beside them on the sidewalk.

"Wait in the lobby for me. I just have to run and park the car," C'Anne said. Novel pulled Rayna inside the building.

"You're in for a real treat, Rayna," Novel whispered inside her ear. "You've never gotten to see me work out on a StairMaster before, have you?"

Rayna stared dully into Novel's eyes.

"Well, it's a sight you won't soon forget," Novel said, laughing.

C'Anne ran breathlessly into the building. "Let me just check us in and then we'll be ready."

As C'Anne acted as tour guide, pointing out what they needed to know about the restrooms, lockers, and showers, Rayna remained silent. She undressed, though, and changed into the exercise outfit C'Anne threw to her. She moved where they told her to move.

C'Anne led them to the StairMasters first.

"All right." Novel smiled. "I'm in my element now."

C'Anne demonstrated how to use the machine. Novel was already warming up. Rayna lifted her legs dutifully on the narrow black strips. Thirty minutes later, sweating and out of breath, the women left the walking machines and decided to try the weights.

First Novel led them in several stretching exercises on the shiny wood floor. Then, they moved on to conquer the machines.

"I think the machines conquered us," C'Anne said, laughing as they left the weight room panting and drenched with sweat.

"This is always a good time for a couple of laps around the track," Novel suggested. C'Anne shrugged.

The women walked up the stairs to the track. All three of them began to run at an easy pace. Though Rayna chose not to talk, Novel and C'Anne discussed politics, hair care, Seattle gossip, and movies. They slowed their pace for the last lap and Rayna seized the opportunity to catch her breath before she stopped running.

"Enough already," C'Anne cried. "If this doesn't get the toxins out of all of our spirits, I don't know what will."

They headed for the showers.

"After you get out of there," C'Anne called out, "let's get in the sauna, then the Jacuzzi."

Rayna stepped into the narrow shower stall and turned the water on cold. She needed something strong enough to break through the gray fog that held her captive. The water hit her skin like pellets. She soaped herself with the peach glycerin soap C'Anne had given her. She threw her head back as the soap slid over her breasts and down her stomach, between her legs, across her shoulders, and under her arms. She soaped her face and neck and as much of her back as she could reach. Then she rinsed herself off and stepped out of the shower and into the sauna.

It was as if she had stepped inside her own womb. The room was dark and moist. She lay on the lower cedar bench. Above her, she sensed C'Anne and Novel, lying naked like her, flat on their backs on the benches. The steam rose and enveloped them.

For the first time in days, Rayna felt the heaviness she had carried since her HIV diagnosis, since Anika's death, lift from her fevered body and swirl around the small room. An incandescent light moved through the mist, and she almost, almost cried out for Anika. Instead she lay still and allowed the tears that wanted to ease from her eyes be released to anoint her, to cleanse her as they moved down her cheeks and nose, dropping onto her rising and falling breasts, glazing a nipple with salt, then falling farther, the tears fell all the way past the well of her navel, into the moist space between her legs, where she would never give birth, but had been reborn in the joys of pleasure, of love, of Theodore gently massaging her with his latex glove. She held herself there in the darkness, in that stillness with her friends.

C'Anne climbed from the upper berth and grabbed Rayna's hand. Silently, she pulled her out of the darkness of the sauna into the blue light of the Jacuzzi.

All three of the women slowly entered the small pool. They sat, saying nothing, soaking in the bubbling jetted water, holding hands.

*   *   *

The following Saturday, when Rayna sat at Coulon Park, she did so with a lighter spirit.

She hadn't guessed Anika would be gone so soon. No matter what the doctors had said, Rayna had faith that they didn't always know what they were talking about.

Rayna lay on the cool grass and lightly traced the words in an imaginary headstone:

ANIKA JANIECE WARREN
April 12, 1984–July 1, 1994

A LIGHT AS GENTLE AS DAWN

"I thought we'd find you here."

Rayna didn't respond to Novel's voice or C'Anne's nervous laughter.

Both women dropped to the ground beside Rayna.

"We know how much you loved her, Rayna," Novel said, stroking Rayna's back.

Rayna pressed herself into the earth, her fingers digging into the neat grass. She let the cool ground be the receptacle for the tears she needed to shed.

The women sat with her quietly, C'Anne gently held her hand. When Rayna's sobbing turned to whimpers, then hiccups, C'Anne helped raise Rayna into a sitting position and wiped her eyes, then made her blow her nose into her already damp handkerchief.

"I've been so afraid to look at my own death," Rayna said between honks. "But I couldn't look at Anika's either. I'm such a coward. I don't have half the courage Anika had. I don't want to die."

"You've got all the courage you need, Rayna. And none

of us wants to die. We're all terrified of dying," Novel soothed.

"Anika wanted to be with you," C'Anne murmured. "Mrs. Jenkins told us at the memorial that the days Anika spent with you were probably the best times of her life. You showed her so much love, in spite of everything and everyone."

"I did love her. In the short time I knew her, I came to love her more than myself, even more than my art. My art is important to me but not more important than the people I care about."

"Well, I'm glad to hear it. Now maybe you'll agree to that body art collaboration I want to do."

"Novel, I can't think about that now. I've still got to deal with going back to a life without Anika."

"And don't forget about our homeboy Theodore," C'Anne said. "He was looking pretty lost at the memorial service."

"I said so many horrible things to him when Anika died. And he still wants to be with me," Rayna said sadly.

"He loves you, you know," C'Anne said.

"In spite of everything, I think he does," Rayna said. "But I don't know if I want him in my apartment right now."

"You could always come and stay with me," Novel offered.

"You know we can't be in the same space for over twenty minutes without arguing," Rayna said.

"When you think you feel good enough to argue with me, that's when I'll know it's time for you to go back home."

The women looked at each other through their tears. Rayna held out her arms to Novel. Novel pulled Rayna inside her embrace and C'Anne hugged them both. All three women burst out laughing. Loud and deep enough for Anika to hear.

July 13, 1994

I don't know what that last moment will be like. I don't know if I'll have the strength or courage to face it. But I do know this: no matter what, when I come to that jumping-off place where the two branches of this life meet and separate, and I step off into the air, those who love me will be there, holding my hand, urging me forward and loving me, as I step from the light of this world into the darkness of the next.

acknowledgments

I would like to thank all who offered encouragement during the writing of this book. My attorney, Keven Davis, and my agent, Beth Vesel, offered indispensable suggestions as always, and my first editor, Stephanie Gunning, handled the initial drafts of the manuscript with her typical diplomatic, hardworking manner. Peternelle van Arsdale, my new editor, contributed a wise evaluation of the book and the line-by-line editing that my inner critic craves. Brenda Peterson saved my writing life, and I can never thank her enough.

In addition, I'd like to thank Kurt Amorose, Marita Dingus, Jody Kim, JoAnn Moton, Barbara Henderson, Barbara Thomas, Faith Davis, Amy Laly, Julia Boyd, Marion Rock and Lenore Norrgard for their encouragement and special assistance with the writing of this book.

I want to give my family their props, as they say. Thank you and I love all of you.